Sarah Guppy was born in North London and migrated north to Edinburgh in 2002. She held a range of jobs before moving to Scotland: administration, charity and campaigning work, gardening. After graduating from Edinburgh University with a BA in Humanities & Social Science; she concentrated on short story writing.

EDINBURGH SHORTS

Sarah Guppy

EDINBURGH SHORTS

AUSTIN MACAULEY
PUBLISHERS LTD.

A CIP catalogue record for this title is available from the British Library.

ISBN 978 184963 664 3

www.austinmacauley.com

First Published (2014)
Austin Macauley Publishers Ltd.
25 Canada Square
Canary Wharf
London
E14 5LB

Printed and bound in Great Britain

Acknowledgments

A thank you to I.K.G as well to other writers in The Co-operative of Creative Writers who offered great encouragement and support.

Contents

Tale of Two Halves	11
Alison the Snake Charmer	28
Oranges	41
Barred from the Buroo	42
Chip Shop Philosophy	52
Forever In Blue Jeans	61
French Evolution	66
Lot Errata	83
More To It Than Meets The Eye	100
Mrs. Anderson	112
Pamela and the Beetroot	120
Shit Happens	136
That's Just The Way It Is Baby	144
The Desperate Hours	165
The Photograph	173
Through a Glass, Darkly	182
Yellow Brick Road	199

Tale of Two Halves

Elizabeth Allgood finished painting the front sitting room a deep dark red. She has been at it since that morning when her husband Richard had gone off to the university. Now came critical appraisal of the work round the elegant Georgian room with long sash windows: overall not bad – a few deft strokes here and there. They had somehow managed to get through Christmas and New Year – she didn't know quite how looking back. There had been a few rows with relatives, broken wine glasses and burnt turkey to contend with. Perhaps her guardian angel, the one who she felt she was able to silently communicate with in the odd snatched moment of peace had bestowed some grace or maybe it had been the couple counselling that they had attended. They had spent Christmas at home (they had had to fight for this in the face of relative disapproval) and things had reached a dramatic crescendo during Christmas Eve when Elizabeth, on strike over a lack of appreciation for her many hours of domestic labours in the kitchen, had thrown the half cooked turkey through a window and out in to the silent dark street.

Ceasefire was reached later that evening but relatives had to make do with a rather soggy nut roast instead. But now it was spring, the days were longer. Bright bulbs were out and a cleansing uplifting wind blew through the Edinburgh streets and crescents. She did love her husband but they always seemed to be at each other's throats: during the holidays she had caught herself eyeing the kitchen devil knives with unhealthy interest. Perhaps it was the influence of the passionate opera she was playing flute in at the moment she thought, rinsing her brushes neatly. Half the time she didn't have a clue as to what was going on in her husband's mind. He was naturally reticent and it was hard work getting a firm clear statement of his feelings about anything, let alone his feelings about her and their marriage. Chopping onions in the kitchen she calculated how many hours she would need just to run over a particularly tricky little solo again.

*

Richard Allgood walked past St. Giles in the Old Town's High Street wondering what had motivated some obscure, anonymous person to write *'there is no time'* on the church's grimy green ancient stone walls. The odd thing was that he felt in some strange way that this piece of street philosophy was actually true: he had been lecturing on the forces of globalisation and the way time seemed to be compressed and work intensified for both labour and capital – and all in the name of increased productivity and efficiency. Certainly, he felt he had no time whatsoever for his own research or even hill walking. He was being paid to regurgitate, deliver and perform but he didn't get enough time to think for himself – he couldn't even feel his own body when walking around in the magnetic black hole of campus academia.

Some strange dis-associational physical splitting process happened as soon as one approached the place of learning: reasoned professional mask on, psychological boundaries up and antennae out, eyes averted. *Tush now man he said to himself,* turning in to George Square. *It's not all bad. Got through Christmas intact. Bank manager happy. Decent pair of corduroy trousers, good wife, decent salary, fine wine and cheese in the larder. Promotion soon, may take over his particular section of Social Sciences.*

More money and maybe a chance to go to Mexico later in the year on research. And not yet forty-three. Lucky, clever old little me.

Yet there were disconcerting times when the university, despite its reputation for excellence and splendid Georgian buildings, seemed no more than a vast theatrical set – it was all a Kafkaesque illusion, this pursuit of knowledge, with millions of questions and endless supplies of possible answers. Really there was a little man peddling away furiously below in the ground somewhere, who kept the whole thing going, over seeing the damned discarded bodies of under performing students and tutors who were branded, coded, recorded, sampled, analysed before magically disappearing without trace – sucked in to a giant abyss or undergoing shrinking modifications Alice in Wonderland style – never to be seen as the same person again or just never seen again. Now and then he was aware of some deep restless energy within him, a sense of profound emptiness and yearning which disturbed him, he couldn't understand it at all. He could not find any reason or justification for his feelings.

During the recent counselling he and his wife had undertaken (Elizabeth's idea, he had found the whole thing deeply embarrassing) he recalled a terrifying childhood dream in which he was completely eaten and swallowed whole by a large black bear. After being eaten and churned around the bear's dark cavernous stomach he was spat out magically intact and whole though shaken by the experience. He hadn't wanted to share this with anybody; he alone would make sense of it.

After walking up the stairs, he chatted briefly to colleagues. In the relative privacy of his office on the third floor he noticed that the huge rubber plant he rescued at a rubbish tip needs water and was actually secreting milky rubbery fluid along her stems. Coffee. *Must have caffeine, no good without it.* Sighing heavily, he saw the pile of unmarked essays on the desk with hardly a dent in it. It'll have to be a late night again as he is already having to print out some lecture notes as well as actually lecture. *Oh Christ.* Elizabeth said not to be late tonight as she's making French onion soup. It is their anniversary. She'll be hurt; she knows it's his favourite.

Sipping hot coffee and looking down in the square he noticed a rather beautiful nubile young student with long blond hair. Magnificent arse, like two boiled eggs in a handkerchief. *Oh do shut up Richard,* he says to himself. *You are a privileged middle aged pig. Do you really want to throw your marriage away on some wild affair with a girl young enough to be your daughter? Have a mid life crises in a few years, you cannot afford it just yet mate.* Sitting, he began to read the essays.

Richard stared blankly in to space; he didn't know how long he had been sitting like that, there in his office. Outside the light was fading. He got through the day okay. The lecture went well and no problems with the overhead projector but the terrible pile of essays still needed to be finished off completely. He picked up the phone and called home. Answer phone. He left a brief message. There is no such thing as a shit free existence he knew, but fuck it, he really fancied a pint. He'd have to chance it. In the past she had bitten his head off for not calling when he knew he was going to be late. Locking his office, he walked down Nicholson Street to his local favourite. He doesn't need to be at campus until two tomorrow so he can unwind with colleagues a bit and laugh at the university inter departmental point scoring.

Elizabeth began to feel her anger rising steadily as she looked at the kitchen clock. Seven o' clock. She knew where he'd be: in that strange boozer with all those other dusty academic types. It had happened time and again. She'd spent ages cooking and painting, all the paint brushes and roller were drying off by the kitchen sink. She had been so efficient that she actually had some time to spare to practise the solo. When she played she felt transported elsewhere and didn't have to think too deeply about anything. The flute lifted her and comforted her and there was something terribly certain and permanent about written musical notes. Why did she have to marry such a bloody emotional retard? They had met at university in England and there had been many times when she thought: I just cannot remain married to you; you are hard work emotionally despite your academic prowess. But she had stuck at it. Examining her face in the bathroom mirror, she wondered if there was another woman or some fresh gorgeous ok –yah Henrietta type student who accidentally on purpose let her stocking tops show during a tutorial. Stuff like this happened alright. When she felt more confident about herself and appreciated she felt she was still attractive – but right now, despite the smart haircut and subtle make up she felt like a rejected hag. It hurt deeply.

"Where the bloody hell are you, then, Dicky?" she shouted to him on his mobile. Richard attempted an explanation, citing a need to discuss a course delivery with colleagues.

In the background noise she heard the chinking of glass and learned banter. Her fury boiled over. She felt physically violent, afraid of what she might do to him as soon as he stepped in through the door. What he was doing was so cruel and thoughtless. Screw it if the neighbours heard her, tough shit. They had heard enough slanging matches and domestic violence by now, they ought to be used to it.

"I'm tired of hearing your fucking lame excuses! You promised you would be back early today. What kind of a man are you, anyway? I'm not waiting for you any longer, Richard."

She hung up and ate some soup, a headache coming on. She had even put candles out on the table, bought fresh flowers. She cursed her stupidity. Never again will she make this effort. Wait until he gets in, then she'll let him have it. She picked up a plate and hurled it in fury against the wall. And then, pride gone and esteem totally crushed she started to cry bitterly and sadly. She cried so much her nose becomes blocked and she blew it on a tea towel. *You have really blown it now mate,* she murmured to herself. Some deep vast damn of emotion was released in her and she surrendered to the heaving sobs and climbing and collapsing at last in to bed, she fell asleep in her clothes.

*

He returned very late to the flat in Montague Street, drunk out of his mind, knowing he is in trouble but not realising that it was far worse than that. For an educated man he was dangerously like a selfish child. At some point during the night it had started to rain but the combination of wind and rain which for other women might have lent a sufficiently windswept and rugged look to their partner did absolutely nothing for Richard. When he was drunk like this he could really feel something, connect with himself in another way. For years he ridiculed his wife for being green and eco, creating endless arguments and debates over whether it was really worth studiously putting things in compost bins and recycling bins – surely it all ends up in the same place?

Now his moment of revenge had come and in a sudden destructive passion he let himself through the back door and in to the shared garden and wrestled drunkenly with the compost bin. He slipped in the mud and ended up lying face down in rotting vegetation. Hauling himself up and cursing under his breath he dragged the compost bin and its contents up the stairs and in to the flat, depositing rotting leaves and mouldy vegetation all over the sitting room floor. Stumbling in to the bedroom he flicked the light on and started shouting in slurred speech. Elizabeth woke with a violent start and then they fought and wrestled each other to the ground. She managed to scratch his face in rage and disgust: this seemed to shock him and he stared in disbelief at his dishevelled wife. You could cut a knife in the air.

"Get out you bastard and don't come back" she almost spat the words.

"You fucking mad old cow!" He gathered himself up and rummaged around for his sleeping bag and rucksack which he kept in a cupboard in the hall. Staggering, he hauled the whole lot out and slammed the front door shut.

So it was that Richard Allgood, for the first time in his life, knew what it was to have no stable home. What the hell could he do now? His damn pride stopped him from calling on a colleague who he knew lived nearby and he didn't have his credit cards on him or that much cash either. He stank of booze, it would be humiliating knocking on a door asking for a bed or money; chances are the gossip would be all over the department too. At first, in a kind of haze, he wandered around for several hours unaware of everything – even the cold night air. Eventually he collapsed asleep in a doorstep in East Preston Street, only to be rudely awakened by a woman who opened the front door the next morning and who threatened to call the police if he did not remove his stuff and himself immediately. He tried telling her that in fact he was not homeless, he was a professional lecturer, there had been a terrible mistake and no, he was not mad either. This didn't cut much ice with the woman who said she had to go off to work now but that if she still found him there when she got back then she would take action. Richard was gob smacked: he was used to being listened to. It was shocking. The woman had no right to speak to him like that. He would simply walk back to the flat (he had the keys in his pocket), offer amends and an olive branch to Elizabeth.

God, his head ached. He would wait until she had calmed down a bit. It had happened quite a few times before afterall. Scrabbling around in his pocket, he found twenty pounds and some coinage and took himself off on a bus to a greasy spoon in Leith Walk. The bus lurched dangerously about and he felt and heard his stomach complain loudly. In the café people stared at him as they caught the whiff of alcohol. Oblivious to the stares, Richard wolfed down fried eggs and chips and a cheap looking cappuccino. On the bus back he is violently sick much to the disgust and fury of both passengers and the bus driver himself who stopped the bus deliberately and ordered Richard off. He walked to the flat only to discover that the keys no longer fitted. The locks have been changed.

The seriousness of the situation sunk in. She had never done this before. What on earth was he going to do now? His pristine corduroy trousers were crumpled and smelly and he stunk of booze and sick. He still had the mobile. He will just have to swallow his pride and call her. He tried the landline and mobile only to get answer phones. He should be marking essays at this moment. Surely she can't keep this up, he will try later. Thankfully his lecture notes were in his office but he cannot possibly go to work in this state. He needed a good shower. Acutely aware of his dishevelled appearance he walked around trying to find a discrete bench to sit on. Hopefully no students or colleagues would recognise him. Feeling like an outcast, he cannot meet the eyes of passing strangers for fear of what judgement he might have seen.

The precariousness of life on the bread line was no longer to be read about with morbid liberal fascination. No, this was real and terrifying. He noticed a rather disturbing advert for online poker on a side of a taxi displaying a weird hybrid mix of squirrel and an eagle: *what kind of poker animal are you*, it quips. The world suddenly felt bleak, harsh and unforgiving: a world of total winners and losers, a universe of extremes, of dog eats dog – a ruthless game indeed. He tried the numbers again but no luck. Shockingly and without warning he started crying. A wave of fear overcame him – quick, hide the eyes and run for cover. It was now afternoon and he would have to do something drastic to cover his absence at work. He walked to Arthur's Seat under gathering clouds and wondered what on earth he would say.

*

It had been a very long time since Elizabeth Allgood allowed herself the luxury and sheer indulgence of a leisurely bath. But this one took the record; she had been lying in it for four whole hours contemplating. She felt shell shocked, traumatised and at the same time strangely empowered. Something shifted inside her and little surges of unexpected thoughts rose up in her mind. It was distinctly odd. It was while she had been soaking that she had the idea to change the locks. Forgetting about the accumulated washing up and the external world, she ignored Richard's calls and had drifted off in to a half sleep in the tepid water. The housework would still be there even when she wasn't, even when she was dead – so why get your knickers in a twist. She resigned herself to not being the perfect wife or housewife: she would face her unknown future with courage. She hadn't slept at all last night and had watched the coming dawn numbly. Reflecting sadly on the state of her marriage over the years, she remembered there was a dress rehearsal at the Queen's Hall at three, smart black clothing required. There was still the flute and good music to be made with others; an enduring joy.

Looking in the mirror she saw the red swollen marks and blue bags under her eyes. As she has fair colouring it really showed. She'd have to do a paint and patch up job. Happiness returned in rehearsal and she played with deft and able fingers. In the spaces in between the notes she was transported once again on a miraculous musical carpet. After, she bought some wine and crashed out on to the sofa. Dozing off she had an exhilarating yet horrifying vision of herself as some Nemesis or Goddess of Retribution basking in a bath of some red fluid: it was unclear whether it was the red paint or human blood.

Richard walked to the top of Arthur's Seat with his tent and backpack. A sympathetic colleague had discreetly (no questions asked) lent him camping gear. It was lucky he had even been in when Richard called round. The colleague had relatives staying so couldn't put Richard up but was thankfully able to provide a quick shower and toast. It had been a humiliating ordeal knocking on the door though. Better than nothing. Richard was tired of lugging all this stuff round now though. It was spitting again slightly, the ground looked slightly wet. Not many people around. He'd better move fast. He dialled Rosemary the patient department secretary and told her he had badly strained a muscle – he had run for a bus but had instead clashed with some guy on a bike. He would be off for two weeks, terribly sorry and all that. A complete shock. Would provide a consultant's note of confirmation of course ASAP. It had never happened before; as she knows; he's very healthy and fit. The art of clever sounding spin.

Richard erected his tent as it had begun raining. The ground was moist so the poles were easy to drive in to the earth. Some strange March hare madness possessed him. He was not entirely sure he was in control of his faculties any longer. Although he had white lied to Elizabeth on a couple of occasions, he had never told a whopper of a porky pie before. He wondered if Rosemary at the university had believed him. He couldn't quite believe his own audacity. Later, as he lay in his sleeping bag in the gathering darkness the thought occurred to him that he was having some kind of personal middle aged identity crises.

The fear returned. *How did he know he was here?* Once, in a bored moment at work he had googled himself but had found no entries. He did not even exist in cyber space. He couldn't believe that Elizabeth had actually changed the door locks. Gradually, he became aware of the earth under him: it was a living entity surging with life and the rising sap of spring. He has never really allowed anything or anyone to ever support him either physically or emotionally, so the sensation of truly feeling the clods he lay on was new. Surrender to the universe.

On impulse he peeked through the crack in the tent and saw the glittering lights of the iconic city sky line against the deep dark Scottish blue. Silence and endless space. Sleeping, he has a weird dream: he is visited by the ghosts of students past and present in his tent. He is revered as a guru in rabbit skins. One of The Learned, a Keeper of the Knowledge. He is presented with incense, fruit, and holy oil. News spreads of his hermit like existence; he is interviewed on TV and radio and becomes a local celebrity character. The tent becomes a shrine, attracting queues of the faithful and curious. And while Richard slept a large hypnotic and luminous moon appeared, exerting its magnetic pull on the watery fluids both in the ground and in human bodies alike. He was woken early by someone shaking his shoulder.

"Oi, Pal. Everything alright with you?"

It was a Council Environmental Warden in a wine coloured uniform, chewing gum.

"My name's Jim. It's alright pal – you can talk to me. Bust up with your other half is it? Made redundant? I won't go to the police."

The ginger haired warden seemed friendly and understanding as if he has seen this kind of thing often along with the dumped waste, shopping trolleys and trash. Fall out takes different forms. Richard blinked himself awake.

"What? Where am I?"

"You're in a tent on the top of Arthur's Seat, that's where you are pal. What brought you up here, mate? A kind of hobby is it. You ought not to be here you know. There are quite a few nutters around, it's not safe. Someone got mugged just the other week. You smell as if you have been on the booze."

Richard realised that it was quite possible that the warden also thought *he* was a complete fruit cake. Living out in the open you had to develop a tough skin.

"Right first time. Terrible row with my wife. Look, I just need a bit of time to get my head straight, you know. I can't go back as she changed the locks. I wonder, if I gave you some cash would you mind buying some food and bringing it back to me here? I'm bloody starving. I will call my wife again today but she may not have cooled off sufficiently."

The smiling warden seemed satisfied with this and walked off with the cash. Pink stripes appeared in the sky. *Wonder what Elizabeth is up to*, he caught himself thinking. He had never really appreciated the beauty of the sky often enough recently as work has been so demanding and in a sudden passion he started to dig doggedly in the earth with his hands – until there was a substantial hole in the ground. He had a deep animal desire to be encased in the soil, to be held safe and secure in the dark moist depths. He worked at it all morning with his sore bare hands until there was a deep pit. The experience was somehow cathartic, therapeutic. An old Indian gentleman walked by with a small dog and asked what Richard was doing.

"Trying to find myself and some peace" he replied to the man, surprising himself with his answer.

"Very good, very good" the elderly man winked, his face creasing like a walnut. "But do remember we are all inter connected in the big human family and in the universe. God be with you on this day. Never under-estimate the power of thoughts." He bowed his head sagely.

The small dog pissed in a nearby gorse bush and then they both disappeared off over the grassy slope. Richard worked on until the hole was several feet deep. The warden returned, bringing crisps, sandwiches and a bottle of Coke. He wasn't very happy with the pit but had taken a liking to Richard and saw the funny side.

"Not trying to bury yourself, are you? Talk about down in the dumps. Is life really the pits for you at this time?" Jim the warden laughed at his own jokes. The hole can be re-filled; the guy was clearly going through something. He looks academic but probity and decency prohibits further questions. There's a lot of it aboot. Sometimes it's the really clever ones in smart clothes who are the total nut jobs. You'd be surprised at what goes on.

Richard found himself opening up to this complete stranger in a way he had never done before. Previously he had been very self conscious about being English and had half dreaded moving to Scotland for an academic post – but as it happened he had only been called a *white settler* once. He told the warden all about his life and marriage up until that point. Jim talked about his own marital problems with his second wife and told him not to worry about it pal, it was common. With a flash of insight, Richard saw how self absorbed his existence had been. He had erected the tent inside the pit so that just the top of the tent was visible. Glancing up at a tree he saw a crow pecking at a thread which had caught a nearby pigeon's claw. The crow was deliberately trying to release the fluttering stuck pigeon.

Maybe that old Indian walnut man was right, maybe we are all inter-connected, and there are many forms of intelligent conscious life. That night Richard again dreamt under the subtle ethereal music of the stars. This time he travelled out of his body and visited people from his

London past. He saw through walls, and heard people's thoughts and re-ran scenes – finally falling back totally in to himself. He then came face to face with millions of worms burrowing in to his tent. Unafraid, he mutated slowly in to a giant worm and found the dark world of soft soil and varying vibrations comforting. Then everything became dark.

Elizabeth Allgood had become aware of the possibility that she was *not* entirely perfect or good – and that it was, in fact, entirely human and alright *not* to be a perfect wife or saintly self sacrificing woman. Struggling to make sense of the last two freakish, turbulent weeks she had once again sought the aid of a counsellor who'd listened compassionately. Richard called again on numerous occasions but she steadfastly ignored him. She felt deep pockets of energy opening up inside her and had, on a sudden whim, daubed the immaculate painted red walls in the flat with yellow clumsy splodges. It was all curiously satisfying. Her chamber orchestra colleagues were politely concerned but had (thankfully) not pried deeply in to the state of her marriage. After the last performance of the opera which went well, she had felt compelled to gather small white feathers on The Meadows. No reason required.

And that night, that memorable rain filled April night, *she* now dreamt she saw a staring giant eye in the bedroom ceiling. Disturbed, she wondered whether this was *her* final descent into madness or whether this was some kind of sign or calling. Waking, she is filled with the awareness of the enormity of the universe and her small, insignificant place within it. Vulnerability in the face of the unknown and in the intense isolation of modern western existence. Gazing at the eiderdown with its miniature valleys and hills she is overwhelmed by the sheer numbers of choices she had about what to do with herself this day.

Her feet took her to Portobello and she washed her tired exhausted face in the sea. Walking restlessly around the nearby streets filled with catkins and emerging sticky buds she came across a small boy of around four or five who shyly indicated that she should follow him if she would like to buy a cake. He then ran off around a street corner. Turning briskly in to East Brighton Crescent, Elizabeth saw three small children selling little fairy cakes and trinkets on a ready made stall in front of a rather grand looking house. Touched by their efforts at cake making and the stall's charm, she bought a few cakes. "Have you got any children?" one little girl asked giving her change from a biscuit tin. The innocent question touched her to the core. She missed Richard. It seemed like an eternity since she had seen him. In his last message he said he was sleeping rough but that he was getting by with the help of a friend called Jim who was letting him stay at his place on some nights for a shower and a bit of grub. He had also said he was sorry about what happened and that he wanted to talk to her.

They met by accident a week later in a local supermarket. At first Elizabeth didn't recognise him; he had a decent beard and his face seemed different somehow, softer. Shyly, awkwardly, Richard spoke with her by the breakfast cereals and pressed his hand in to hers. He spoke in a strange new language, saying that he had been a Dick right enough, that he'd been asleep both to himself and to her but that things were different now. He moved back in to the flat and politely insisted that he hang a piece of dried gorse on a wall: "a reminder of the black wildness" he muttered – but she didn't enquire further.

There was something about the trees in George Square –
timeless yet full of character. Returning to work, Richard
felt grateful for the good everyday things in his life. Far
from being in thrall to some God of Reason, he now
believed that life was more to do with equilibrium or
balance between reason and emotion. It always had been so
since antiquity and always would be so. Elizabeth realised
that relationships were a bit like music in that both were as
much about the gaps and silences in between as about the
actual notes and words. One didn't need to control the
words or notes or count them; it was part of an overall
pattern. The compost bin once again took pride of place in
the back yard. *Blessed are the cracked for they let the light
in.*

Alison the Snake Charmer

Keeping a pet guinea pig has probably never been seen as the epitome of normal femininity but Alison Mode has long stopped worrying about that. Not that she ever really conformed anyway. She always finds the feminine hygiene sections in chemists slightly intimidating in their oh so very pristine efficiency. No, she has more immediate and banal questions on her mind right now – questions and puzzles about why the seeds she's sewn the summer just gone haven't done what they were supposed to do on the packet. They haven't germinated and on top of this flowers that for years bloomed one colour now bloomed a starkly different hue. Looking back maybe it was an omen of some kind, a warning about bad seeds. Spock nestles up in his well ventilated hutch, watchful eyes and ears nearly always at the ready. He's a big black haired bugger of a guinea pig and he's successor to Kojak – another balding guinea pig who had sadly died two years previously.

"Spock! Have you been at that big bag of gripo nuts, pal? I just bought them too. Is this what I get for letting you have a run around. That's the trouble these days isn't it, nae respect anywhere at all. And who cleans out your box? Lucky I didnae leave ma TV dinner out for your second course, eh?"

Spock looks on impassively, his wee grunting squeals over for today. For Alison these creatures are literal life savers, confidantes with integrity who never ratted on her or betrayed her secret real feelings. And lord knows she's learnt the hard way about being discerning about who you share your inner most feelings with. Alison's no social butterfly, flittering about on Flatter, the newest social networking site to take the universe and her Restalriggs estate by storm. Restalriggs, a poor relation of Edinburgh's Leith, has great blocks of not totally inhuman housing: there is greenery, human diversity and rather stylish diamond shapes cut in to frontage. Alison's lived here all her life; she grew up in this very flat. The TV dinner bubbles up in the microwave as grey globs of rain smack roads with force. She's due in for a shift at the home at three; she'll try and be brave and take the pack of cards and maybe oranges in come hell or high weather.

The Harbours private care home for the elderly sits solidly on The Grange in Marchmont. A very large late Victorian house, it undoubtedly once housed servants, masters and maybe a school mistress. Ruth O' Connor, indisputably the Manageress or Mistress of this establishment cut a formidable presence amongst the five residents and her five care staff. Prints of kittens and bowls of fruit adorn walls; ash trays a long lost taboo. It's evening bath time for all and upstairs English world war two veteran Fred Branch is trying it on with young lassie Karen, who's been assigned to helping him wash. Most of the time Fred shuffles around in slippered depressive gloom; female flesh appears to be the only antidote to his condition.

"Don't you be messing with my medals, girl. They mean something you know. Now do let me have a little peck and please don't scrub so hard with the soap. You keep my secret and I'll not tell Ruth about the secret fags you and Michelle steal out in the yard. *Deal or no deal?*"

"Is that old boy Fred chatting you up again, Karen? Don't let him worry you hen. I should tell you he stuffed the cooked veg down his pants, it was that much of a hit with him. He's been grumbling all day, calling Alison shorty even when they were at the cards."

Joan Murdoch, another resident, is calling out in sympathy from bathroom number two where another young lassie is trying her level best to shampoo her key client's hair. Joan maintains a fondness for the Marcel Wave and indeed different kinds of hair wave so staff are kept busy often with the rollers. It has been a helpful ice breaker though, a topic of conversation that Alison, new staff member, had managed to strike up with Joan. For it is rapidly becoming apparent to Alison that you need all the allies you can get in this place, this place where care is not the only thing that's dished out. She's been working at *The Harbours* for a month, having completed her SVQs at night. It is late September and next week it's Joan's birthday. Tentatively, Alison suggests to Ruth that there be a day out in The Botanic Gardens if the weather was good. Doubtfully eyeing Alison's colourful head scarf, Ruth said she'll think about it. The syrupy glucose medication finally washes out of Fred's shirt as Alison completes her washing rota. She'd ignored Karen loudly asking for a *fanny pad* during late afternoon break. *Don't complain, but don't be too different either* as some won't like it, her poor ma had said before she died. It's a fine dangerous line she concludes; switching off the TV at the appropriate time. Stewart, Alice and Rose, the remaining three residents appear to be engrossed in *Resident Evil.* She has a feeling she might have to resort to tricks with eggs or oranges after all.

Sunlight bounces off vast panes of glass in the Royal Botanic Gardens' greenhouses. As a wee lass Alison and her ma visited the famous Gardens and admired the rockeries, flowing stream and the epic efforts of nineteenth century Botanists on quests to document and understand unknown plants. It's how she learnt about seeds and about being patient and tolerant with things that grow.

"There's that stone dog again, Alison. Isn't it beautiful? I think it's a whippet of some kind. Maybe it's a stone memorial of an actual pet the owners had. A minor miracle that Ruth agreed to this day out you know. I'm gradually coming to the conclusion, Alison, that you are indeed working a kind of personal magic. Are you a white witch?"

Alice, an incredibly intelligent retired barrister is clearly warming to Alison. Alice had noticed the stone dog on the walk way to the Gardens' entrance. She has a walking stick which Alison discreetly keeps an eye on while carrying the packs of sandwiches Big Marg, the in-house cook had earlier prepared. Alison nearly put her foot in it that morning before they left by cracking jokes about big catering tubs of margarine, but quickly rescued herself. All this selected emphasis on political correctness and anti discrimination was both empowering and stifling. Then, to top it all off, the irony: Big Marg nonchalantly called Fred the infamous Cold Meat Salad. And all this delivered in the kitchen whilst biting in to a cake. *Oh yes*, Alison knew all about the yawning gap between polite rhetorical ideals and harsh lived realities, for Alison Mode is actually a dwarf. Little Person, LP, midget, freak – she'd been called them all. Ema Jewska, Deputy Manageress of *The Harbours*, wheels Stewart ahead of them while gracefully fending off questions from both Karen and Michelle who either don't want to see how intrusive they are being or who don't care.

"How come you look so young then? Don't they have free contraception in Poland like here?

"I wish I could get away with wearing a shorter skirt like that. I've got to lose some weight first though."

Ema, a kind hard working Polish lady simply doesn't see the hidden motivations that fuel the hounding questions. When they joke about killing for a figure like Ema's there's uneasiness in the air; her colleagues are not really interested in who she is or how she is. It's awful to overhear. Ema has lots of professional qualifications and had the initiative to suggest they all go and see some free art in Inverleith House.

"You don't eat much during the day do you, is that how you keep so slim? My ma says you ought not to eat carbs after three. Did you go away over the weekend then like you said?"

Ema stutters out some replies, trying to focus on Stewart who can only communicate with the aid of a device which looks like a type writer placed on his lap. A *speak-a-metre;* she'd joked to a stony faced Ruth. Fred, weighed down with medals, trails behind Alison and Alice on the look out for a bit of skirt. Poor love, he'd had the blues ever since his beloved drowned in Portobello open air swimming pool, back in the 1930s. He'd even been a journo-hack back then, a budding poet. And this before he'd seen action in North Africa.

Party hats quiver, jelly trifles wobble and tea is slowly slurped and smacked amongst teeth both real and unreal. Joan is having an open air field day as are they all as the bemused café staff look on wondering perhaps that the only missing ingredients from this scene might be a modern Mad Hatter or dopey dormouse. Before tea Ema, Alice and Rose had traipsed off to see the Art in Inverleith House. Dropping a lump of sugar in a tea cup, Alice cuts to the cross examination The café is on a raised grassy mound; it's a fine day with warm air with quite a crowd seated inside and out.

"My dear gal, you say it's Art with a Capital A but frankly all I see is the painting of a hyper child. There *is* no art or method in it. You say he's an up and coming Artiste from Hungary, the former Eastern bloc. Well, that may be. It's just as well it was free to be fair."

This direct line of attack is aimed at Ema whose only defence is that she thought seeing The Art might "be a fun thing to do". What is it with these Brits, who love Legalism and who have to have a 'reason' for everything? Ema muses; grateful that at least she is not the only creative outsider or minority group. Since arriving in Scotland three years ago, she'd noticed great play is made of being entrepreneurial and independently minded – but not *too* independent. Alison stands out too for all too obvious reasons and even dares to wear what looks like exotic Muslim headdress. Late summer wasps make bee lines for dollops of jam lying glistening in the sun.

Alison's asking for trouble maybe – but still Ema's curious as to how exactly such a person could practically qualify as a legitimate Carer. And why on earth does Alison keep rummaging at her sleeves, they seem to be full of *some thing.* Rose, a more gentle unassuming soul who had been named after her namesake some ninety three years ago, eats her fair share of cake while quietly watching some sparrows enact their very own kind of pecking order. Stewart seems content with Karen's Word Search skills while Michelle sexts on her mobile, relieved that Fred's amorous adventure had come to an end. *A hard on at ninety!* Michelle never thought it physically possible, being as she is in thrall with youth. Fred had spotted a pretty old biddy by some late flowering shrub and the genteel chase had been on. Fred could power-walk with the best of them right enough.

"I think it's time for a wee spot of nature's free magic."
Alison announces suddenly, thinking the time ripe.

Magic tricks proved a wise fruitful remedy to early bullying: if you skilfully played in to clichés about circus freaks then you silenced the snide in advance. You could then clobber your tormentor with a single line, as though you'd earned the right somehow. Alison juggles five oranges high in the air to claps and jeers, these are silenced though when a single orange is dropped and rolls off down the mound. And that's not the only thing to fall flat: in his haste to rescue the errant orange, Stewart alas has fallen forward on to his face. His wheelchair is the latest design with a self – driving turbo switch. The afternoon collapses in calamity and with rising dread some in this party know they will have to provide answers.

Leaves are beginning to fall signalling slow change. They begin to dot the lawn with colour and a macabre yet stately monkey tree out in *The Harbours'* back garden is both strangely beautiful and grotesque all at once. Perhaps a lot of life is like this. Ruth O' Connor is used to being whispered about behind her back – that's the price you pay for getting to the top. A trained nurse, she'd completed her training at Edinburgh's best institutions. Her parents were Irish and moved from Paisley to Edinburgh during the war. *Irish sounding surname, Jewish sounding Christian name*: *funny mix* trainee doctors had quipped, bored on the wards. But no more odd or funny than her Polish sub-manager, who despite *her* surname is actually Catholic. A clock beats steadily in Ruth's office: listening to it helps steady her building fury.

"Can you please both explain to me what on earth Stewart was doing lying flat out on the grass? Alright, so there are no visible cuts or bruises. He was shocked and clearly upset though as was the manageress of the Café who saw the incident. You say you were juggling oranges, Alison. But as far as I'm aware *such talents* are not the most important for this job."

The accused stand side by side, perhaps in only temporary solidarity. Best just be honest and apologise, *take ownership* was the latest buzz concept in the many training manuals they'd both had to read in Warsaw and in Edinburgh. Ema holds her and Alison's ground politely.

"I was surprised as everybody else Ruth but I don't think any serious damage has been caused and up until his fall Stewart was actually laughing away as they all were. It was good to see them having fresh air and fun at no great expense too as I'm aware of accounts. You were saying just the other day that you wanted them to get out more and do activities rather than just watch TV."

Experience has taught Alison not to argue and quibble over the word *incident. What is your problem, love?* she thinks. It was a relatively minor accident in her book. Speaking of books and definitions; she'd have to consult her own at home. Maybe while Spock has his daily run-a-round. Maybe it's her imagination but Ruth O'Connor's eyes look snake like in the gloom.

"Look as well as being a trained Carer I'm also a fully trained up magician and I know it makes some really happy to watch magic and such like on TV. But I thought I could teach them some card tricks, small safe things. You know, to stimulate them."

"Are you saying both of you that you don't think the residents are actively learning enough? Or that they suffer from some awful form of group depression? How else am I to take this implied criticism of my management? Yes, I do recall commenting on Fred's permanently dour face. And yes, there are times when *The Harbours* could do with activities outdoors perhaps." Ruth sighs, weighing up what's been said. She continues.

"Alright, so this is a verbal caution to you both at this stage as I simply cannot afford and nor can the Governing Board afford potentially libellous complaints from irate relatives. I'm sure you both know how easy it is to lose reputation. I'm open to the idea of some creative activities as long as they are supervised. That is all."

The absolved glance briefly at one another and leave for their respective homes. Travelling home on the bus, Alison recalls with a start where she'd seen a similar look: in the eyes of a poisonous green mamba snake. She really isn't sure if Ruth means what she says.

A pink dawn develops over Restalriggs; most folk are fast asleep. But not Alison Mode; she has a calling. The well thumbed Journal – hyphen – Dictionary lies casually open on 'P' and poisons by her sitting room window. Spock *is* asleep though and had earlier scoffed an enormous number of onion wots-its that she'd stupidly left lying open by the sofa. He's already caned the gripo nuts; quite where he put all the grub she didnae know. She'd only been out the room for five minutes max visiting the loo and, what with all the hoo har at work, she'd forgotten what a fast little mover and shaker the furry blessed bugger is. Crumbs are distributed all over the freshly hovered carpet: *great.* Thankfully she only works at *The Harbours* part time – her other missing hours are spent conducting house visits both for Council and for a separate private agency. Yet other wee stolen hours are snucked in here and there where and when she can for her own personal development and for studying. Alison has made up her mind that she must *do* some thing to test the waters in the home. All the residents look permanently depressed and withdrawn, it's disturbing.

"So Spock, what do we do now? How to smoke out any enemies and see true motives. Time for a snaffle and smalt I think. Something to get the old mental tea leaves going when challenged. Some may say Spock; nae they *do* say that I'm daft and that I'm funny in the head. But between you and me and the Sneezewood, pal, I know when something's fishy and not quite right."

The Sneezewood is the very special wooden thinking stool; an item of furniture that once belonged to her darling mother who'd died in a care home far less luxurious than *The Harbours.* And it is on this stool that Alison now sits out her very best thoughts that design ways out of tight spots. She twists metal coat hangers in to interesting shapes as she susses people out. It's a habit she's mastered well. As a young girl, her ma had emphasized the cleverness of dwarves; they'd read Germanic tales of remote forests and small wise people who often worked metal and earth to good effect. Her mother passed away in an awful home in awful circumstances over twenty years ago; staff said she'd slipped in the bath — but then Barbara Mode wasnae supposed to have been left unattended even briefly towards the end of her life. Barbara was average height and 'normal' looking — whatever 'normal' really ever means. Then there were Alison's abysmal photographs taken on her mobile phone on the sly in the home; this was before Barbara died. Photos of grime, dust and gremlins both seen and unseen. It was horror right enough, horror both real and imagined.

Yeah, what ever Spock. Later pal. You scoff my food then sleep it off pal. The wee beastie stirs briefly in his sleep. The trusty faithful Dictionary-Hyphen-Journal will help steer her way through. When Barbara died, Alison's best friend died also and the grief was over powering, crippling almost. She hadn't gone out the house for months. A kind doctor and work colleague saved her and suggested she get a pet. It was either that or go mad continuing to trace her hands on walls with biros. Sometimes it was the only way she knew she was alive and was living. It was somehow an inevitable step to then invent a whole new language *Quibblon* which helped to de-code, translate and uncover lies, smokescreen and half truths uttered in the name of political correctness and smug self preservation. Spock and *Quibblon* saved her sanity at the time and made her laugh when she thought she'd forgotten how.

Alice, Joan and Rose are playing at cards: at *Grey Flutter* to be specific; an off shoot of *Beggar My Neighbour*. Alison helps Stewart complete a cross word; he loves her company and taps out wit on the speak-a-metre which she enjoys but is careful not to laugh at too loudly as management may conclude it uncouth. For uncouth is reserved for youth apparently. A small plaster remains on Stewart's forehead; otherwise he's right as rain from his fall over a month ago. The Home GP visited, relatives visited and then the drama subsided in to distant memory. Outside, it's windy and the days are short. Rose sneezes rather loudly; her eyes have been streaming throughout the game.

"It's my hay fever again. I thought I'd be spared but no. Excuse me. There must still be pollen in the air. My turn again girls – now play fair."

"My dear gal, why don't you ask what's-her-face to bring you a box of tissues from upstairs? That is what they are paid to do after all not sit around and gossip. It's quite likely dust as I'm not sure they clean as they are supposed to also do."

Alice's voice cuts across the room like finest Scottish rock crystal glass. She's aware of what she's just said though for even working and retired barristers slip up. Her eyes glance nervously towards Alison. She doesn't think much of any of the staff except for Alison and Ema who she has time for because they both exhibit independence of thought. When Alice first arrived at *The Harbours* over five years ago she'd had several loud screeching matches with Ruth. Ruth O' Connor is due in shortly and Alison has a plan. A guided fumbling through the *Quibblon* led her to a simple three part remedy and the timing is about right as Fred's depressive gloom and the ladies' barely disguised apathy and boredom fill the room.

What is the longing at the root of the envy was the wisdom Alison had re-read on Page 73 only last night. And this reign or regime must change somehow. It's a risk right enough but she couldn't bare to see the suffering any longer and she refused to have the very life sucked slowly out of her too. *What kind of quality care was this for all concerned?* Turning her head briefly to greet all in the room; Ruth steps in to her office and as she does so she catches Alison audaciously juggling eggs, of all things. Eggs which slip, then crack messily upon the floor. Cue Spock, released from the tunnel of Alison's sleeve. Loud hysterical screams of *it's a huge rat* as Spock squeals round the unknown room. The beastie heads out for the kitchen and there's a clattering of pans from in there too. Big Marg unlocks the back door just as Alison planned and it's then that the strategically placed sniblet of butter on the door step works its wonders as a frightened Ruth slips on an ankle. *Break an egg to break a leg* roars a delighted Fred but even more amazing than this is the way Ruth's hard lined face crumples in surrender.

Fred, it transpired, suddenly remembered, as if by some kind of magical process of osmosis occurring between people, the odd bit of German from his days seeing action in North Africa. *Wunderlicht,* he'd said; gazing at Alison as if she truly is a pint size messiah come to save the residents from eternal hell on earth. *You are a kind of wunderlicht;* just like the mysterious African moons he'd seen years ago. He's recently taken pen to paper again; able to deal with a long dead wife better now somehow. Ruth's off duty with a severely sprained ankle. She'd looked like a ship lost at sea, the buttering up has decimated her. All traces of poisonous venom seemed cast out for now and Ema Jewska is on call for most probably the next six weeks.

Six whole sacred weeks; a chance maybe to plant different kinds of seeds. Keen to set an example, Ema is out in the back garden planting bulbs, despite it being All Hallows Eve or All Souls. *Glunk* is the term Alison enters in to the good old book back at home. Inspired by a new kind of Fred; it describes a new kind of clumsy gentleman hunk. Orange paper lanterns hang from the lower branches of the Monkey tree. Even more mysterious than the visible manifestations of the moon Fred said, are the sometime dark hidden underside workings of the moon. One couldn't have the visible without the invisible. *Day care just got more caring* pipes Big Marg; placing party rings and sausage rolls out for them all. They can bob the apples later.

Oranges

Written by Fred, resident of *The Harbours*

Zestful and succulent
Round rinds, oval orbs
Pick thick this cellulite skin
And tangy fragrance:

Revealing mounds to gorge
Upon the juicy spreading segment flesh.
Cut flush out the poison
And pithy pip squeaks

Reintroduce the juice and
The life giving squirt
Of popping acid octopus stain.
Shock of colour,

Hard pills evacuated
Submerge teeth,
baptize being
In to this simple wonder.

Barred from the Buroo

It was not the first time that month that Margaret Ferguson wondered about the two burly security guard men guarding the doors at the Job Centre Plus complex. Job Centre *Plus.* It sounded like an outsize clothing outlet; like an elasticated underwear range. Like you were getting something extra here, some extra bit of efficient enhanced service or that *you,* as claimant or dependent user were expected to give a bit extra – you know – go the extra super human mile to get a job even if there were no jobs actually out there. And what exactly was to be so heavily guarded – public funds? Sitting and waiting to be interviewed, Margaret thinks that it smacks a bit of enforcement, mistrust, surveillance. She's sitting upstairs on the first floor of a large building and one of the security guards had actually phoned up on his CB phone or whatever it was – to tell another guard on the second floor that she, a person, a somebody, a Margaret was about to come upstairs to be interviewed.

Talk about traffic control and crowd management techniques. The woman who sits opposite her is her allocated advisor Maureen Cameron. She wears a large gold cross and taps information in to her PC. Years ago, when Margaret's da had been unemployed in the thirties – she'd heard him refer to the Unemployment Assistance Bureau or Labour Exchange. He said he was "on the buroo" and signing on as he was unable to find any work. It had been difficult enough wading through all the official forms that asked detailed questions about her widow's pension, her own pension, her income – no wonder she's now feeling a bit crabbit. The pile of completed forms sits in front of

Maureen now and the vast open plan office seems harmless and bland with grey walls. Maureen shuffles the papers and looks searchingly at her.

"Mrs. Ferguson, I'm afraid you don't have enough National Insurance contributions to claim Job Seeker's Allowance. Although you were working for many years as was your late husband, it appears there are several years just prior to your retirement in fact where there is a contributions shortfall. And anyway, you are a highly unusual case in that you are officially retired from the state's point of view and from the DWP's perspective. You claim your own state pension which is sufficient and on top of this you receive a widow's pension. Most folk look forward to a well earned retirement and yet you say you want to work at sixty nine. You must surely be aware that we are in the midst of a deep recession and that there's stiff competition for jobs. Frankly, you can offer extensive retail experience but are clearly not computer literate. Can I suggest that you instead take up a hobby or activity which will get you out of the house and socialising and keep you fit and active? Edinburgh is crying out for volunteers; I'm sure there will be something for you."

Margaret feels a hot flush of anger as she stands up in front of the desk, all five feet one inches of her. Her very own Jack the brickee, her deceased other half, affectionately referred to her as the half way hoose. She may be short, but heck she's feisty. How patronising, talking about taking up a hobby. The advisor made her sound like a demented lonely old cow; she feels like giving the woman a Niddrie half brick about the face, like.

"Eh'm on me own now, hen and anyway – thir's nae jobs t'pursue but I need to live, same's you. Eh'm just bored out of ma poor wee heid and I really don't need any of your put downs. Ah worked respectably for longer than you and ah would a thought The Government would be wantin' folk to work and the like but your colleague at the Dalkeith office goes on about the dependency ratio and tax burdens and such like nonsense and now you."

Stomping out of the High Riggs office, she walks along a rainy Grassmarket. *Aw Christ, eh'm thorough drookit but what's a wuhman tae dae?* She dives in to a café for comfort and tea.

They had spent some of their happiest hours in The Whithoose. The Whithoose Pub at least that's what they called it then. Not *their* hoose mind, nor even in the nearby big posh Niddrie Hoose which some locals were afeared of with its forbidding seventeenth century chimneys. No, it was drinking and mingling in The *White* Hoose that they, Jack and Margaret, had been at their canty best. This was before their son Douglas had been born in the early sixties and well before he finally emigrated to Australia in the eighties, sick of the riots in Niddrie and the gloom of recession. It was the fifties then and Margaret wore petticoats and big rayon shiny dresses and Jack often finished early on a Friday so Margaret would wait with the other lassies outside the deco drinking hole, all tarted up. The Whithoose used to be a roadside Inn in the 1930s when there were growing numbers of cars on the roads right enough. Very stylish it was and is: all clear white and green and smoke and mirrors.

The Niddrie brick factory was literally just a bus ride away or you could walk it in twenty minutes or so. Margaret still has a Niddrie brick in her flat; Jack nicked it when they moved in together. You could get a cheap cocktail in The Whithoose; it was the place to be seen. Lassies that were too familiar with the laddies at too young an age very quickly got a reputation and were not always asked to dance. *Clatty bint* was what such girls were called. But the drinkin' dancin' and romancin' in the elegant Whithoose was right braw enough and as a young married couple they often returned to their small flat above the lingerie shop in Niddrie Mains Road for more wee Friday night cocktails served at their own private formica bar.

Margaret worked in the lingerie shop for over twenty years; and in all those years the wee darkee coloured doll hadn't been moved from the shop window's central display cabinet. Fashions in underwear had come and gone over the years in *Blustons Lingerie* but the shop window display remained eerily stagnant as if some mass cultural mind set was unchanged through both Labour and Conservative administrations – indeed through booms and every kind of bust. There had been security then though; security in jobs and in underwear that securely and demurely held in female flesh. You knew where you were with things then. Good was good and bad was bad. Not like now though, eh. Margaret muses now waiting for a bus home. Some of the wee young lasses she'd seen up at the toon on a Saturday night! And *no* friggin' jobs out there; you had to make one yourself, like. Speeding past masses of golden daffodils in Niddrie, she remembers she'd still not mastered the mobile phone Douglas had bought her for Christmas when he'd been over. *Barred from the friggin' buroo at her age.* Oh, the utter shame of it, to be old, retired *and* redundant. She couldn't face telling anyone about all this but some how there had to be a way out of it, eh. She lets herself in to the wee flat at the main door stair.

A horrible sense of déja vu almost hovers in mid air in the GP's consulting room. Margaret sits on one side of yet another official desk – this time the desk of Dr. Christine McTulloch who often means well but doesn't ever seem to have the time to really listen to her. The surgery looks friendly enough with humorous posters encouraging patients to eat five a day, give up smoking, take up exercise, take family planning seriously. As she sat in the waiting room area she remembered again the bizarre call from the Inland Revenue out of the blue asking if she was the only resident at the flat and asking if she could confirm her age and retirement.

An anonymous man had called from some tax office in Glasgow; his voice flat and dull. When she answered all his questions he just thanked her and rang off. It left her feeling as if she'd committed some crime. And sitting here today in Dr.McTulloch's consulting room wanting more anti-depressants; Margaret wonders at how the entity called 'the British state' could appear at one moment intrusive and big brother like – at another kind, concerned and parental.Dr. McTulloch carefully records Margaret's blood pressure and weight in a file. At least on this official record though mention was made of her subjective inner life, her feelings – at Job Centre Plus she was stripped of her identity, having been filed in claims section A-F.

"Margaret, I'm happy to sign one more course of Prozac to you which will last six months – but beyond this I'm very concerned about just signing off endless prescription notes. It's not really a permanent and long lasting solution. You seem depressed and isolated and I completely understand that you feel unable to cope with every day life since your husband died. Nevertheless, I'd really encourage you to join some social groups – maybe walking groups or gentle exercise or maybe helping out at your local community centre or church. You need company to take your mind off all these negative thoughts you have been describing to me. If you like I can look in to bereavement counselling groups if you feel that will help."

"Dr. McTulloch, ah feel alright most of the time I just get weepy in the mornings and *ma heid's mince* cos eh'm missing my Jack, that's all. Eh'm not sure that eh'm "suffering from clinical depression" – that sounds a bit like a label tae me. All I dae know is that ah have me ups and downs that's all. You havnae written that down in your wee records – that eh'm crackin' up have you? Ah know my own heid and ah know what makes me feel alright. And yes, I have got plans to get oot and aboot, hen."

The GP smiles at this as they have a good working client-professional relationship. These days she finds her job is more and more about counselling, comfort and just chat rather than actual physical ailments. Dr. Christine McTulloch, a product of a fine London medical school, was much praised for her conversational soft skills with patients but still retained private doubts about the fragility of Margaret Ferguson's mental well being as she shows Margaret the consulting room door. The patient's social circumstances seem grim but her financial condition relatively stable. And, three days later, after Margaret has received some cash from her son Douglas via Western Union; Margaret is shocked to find an unknown woman knocking on *her* front stair door. And on a Sunday morning too. Margaret has heard of the 24 global society, but this is ridiculous.

"Hello, I'm sorry to trouble you, but Dr. Christine McTulloch has recommended that I pay you a visit. I'm Sandra Pickle, your local CPN – that's Community Psychiatric Nurse. I do hope you got my recent letter advising you of my visiting. It's Margaret, isn't it? Do you mind if I come in, would that be alright? I did try calling you on your mobile a few times but got no answer and I gather you don't have Internet connection. And I'm sorry but Christine didn't actually give me your landline number.

Is it convenient to have a quick chat about how things are going?"

Margaret stands shell shocked on the doorstep. This was a different kind of bomb. Now German bombs – well. Sometimes they still dug up the buggers in folks' back yards – there was one found near the Grassmarket jist the other day. *No it bloody isn't okay to come in and have a wee chat lass -what do you think eh am – an on call twenty four hour eejit?* is what she thinks but doesn't quite say out loud as she knows her GP means well. The fact that this Sandra Pickle woman calls her GP by her first name shows her these two are right thick with each other. But this is going way too far. It doesnae feel quite right and some form of drastic action is required; some speaking oot in the name of privacy and decency – ay, and common sense tae. Margaret thanks the woman politely for her concern but says she feels just fine and that no, she got no letter. Saying she will get in touch with Dr. McTulloch next week but thank you she doesn't need any more visits; she politely shuts the front door.

Young skateboarders move fearlessly in Bristow Square. They are bold and full of beans. One young laddie with long hair and a baseball cap seems to almost fly in the air and is parted temporarily from his board – only to be reunited seconds later. They attract a bit of a crowd as they try out their street antics and pigeons scatter, startled by the sudden roll of the wheels and clashing of rubber on pavement. It's been a few weeks since the nightmare out of the blue visit from the CPN; Margaret complained to Dr. McTulloch. The good doctor apologised, reassuring her that she didnae actually give permission for Ms.Pickle to visit her concluding that it must have been an administration error. But the GP was insistent about Margaret getting her exercise and five vegetables a day and here Margaret conceded as it was a kind of trade off.

Watching the lads now; she doesn't know quite how they control their boards; she feels sure they may crash at any minute. *Once I had fine little roller skates as a wee lass and I used to skate up and down ruining the other bairns' chalk hop skotch marks on the paving.* Her da, a Newcraighall miner; had bought them for a distant birthday. How nice to be happy and carefree she muses, walking again to that little greasy spoon café – the same one she'd popped in to the day of the High Riggs saga. That had been a month ago now and she is still recovering from being processed; she hadn't realised what would be involved. She orders a coffee and a bacon roll from the Italian looking proprietor and plops herself down at a table by the window.

Jack had worked faithfully for the Niddrie and Benhar Coal Company right up until 1991 until, sadly, the works closed. The chimneys could be seen for miles around; the site boasted three Hoffman continuous kilns and was responsible for producing bricks that built large swathes of Edinburgh's twentieth century residential buildings. People forgot things like that. In their early courting days she used to meet Jack sometimes at the works once he'd copped off from a shift. They'd steal a tipsy kiss underneath one of the ancient trees in the grounds of Niddrie House; this was amongst the burnt ruins of the house. You can still see a few old trees amongst the modern estate if you look hard enough. In the winter it got very dark but you could still see the men coming out of the brick works in huddled groups; their thick coats reeking of smoke and industry.

In the last few weeks Margaret had taken herself off in near desperation to the nearby local drop in Community Learning Centre. Well, she had to do something with hersen; the word 'redundant' was just so awful. And she'd tried explaining to *that* information advisor at the learning centre that she hadnae got a clue as to how to operate a computer, like. She thought a mouse was a wee furry beastie and the lady laughed which was alright. She'd explained the problems she'd had claiming benefits and mentioned her GP's advice and consequently she'd gone on a couple of wee local walks with other old fogeys. It had actually been quite interesting, almost as if seeing familiar places through new eyes. Now there was an activity that naebody could deny her: if there is a right to work then there's surely a right to walk. And the walking and friendly chatting cleared her mind a bit and she got to wear her new breeks.

"What's the matter, my lady? Are you having a bad day? Can I get you something nice like some cake to cheer you up?" The café proprietor wipes and clears her table; he'd seen her wistful look.

"I just cannae find work and eh' m not going out enough I don't think. My husband died a year ago and it really hit me, it did. I've been slowly recovering; trying to get on with my life the best way I can with or without the government's help like." She gets up to go then, putting on her coat. Recently the weather had got warmer and she's due to meet the community walking group again today for a trip round the Botanic Gardens.

"What's that you say? You looking for a little job and some extra cash and company? I could do with some help in the kitchen – cooking, cleaning, washing up. I can pay you cash. Say a couple of days a week."

He looks genuinely interested in her, no bullshit put downs or polite sounding small talk. *It will get me oot of the damn hoose anyway,* Margaret thinks. And it might be fun. *Fun.* She's forgotten the meaning of that word too. She takes his business number and says she needs a day to think about it. And a distant memory of fun takes her back to the lads in Bristow Square instead; a place where her shortness could be an asset when riding and cruising on skateboards. Stuff the sensible community walk; all work and no play had made her Jack a dull laddie on occasion. One skate boarding lad's fair game and suddenly, Margaret finds herself trying to stay on his board and nearly falling over. Lucky she's wearing her breeks, eh. *Never mind,* she says to the lad. *Ah'l not give up yet; the fight hasnae left ma body completely pal. Never mind any of it, eh. The JSA can take a flying hike up someone else's jacksie.*

She takes out a can of Iron Bru and gives the laddie a sip. Always take pride in yourself; that's what her Jack said. She'd taken to always carrying a can of Iron Bru around or two alongside the secret stash back home in the fridge that the doc need not know aboot. That was one five-a-day she couldnae dae withoot. *Aye,* thinks Margaret giving the board another try. So what if ah falls on ma bahooky, I have always been able to laugh at myself. With practice anything could be possible and you can bar me from one buroo pal – but you'll no take ma Iron Bru.

Chip Shop Philosophy

文革

Build castles in the air but don't move in

Looking at the sand castles and forts from a distance will help you, Gina. You will achieve perspective on your place in the wider universe. That is what Professor Tommy Ling-Wei said to his only beloved daughter years ago on Portobello Beach. *You must do many things in life to live well and fully: learn also to minimise within the mind, think miniature Bonsai tree when you are raging like a dragon possessed. Do not give your enemies or those who wish you harm in whatever shape or form – don't give them weapons. Above all else be tolerant and before you criticise another, look first at yourself.* Gina was only eight at the time and her father's philosophy – or was it the people's philosophy – she wasn't sure – had only been heard in part.

She was more interested in swimming underwater and looking at the pretty white-pink jellyfish as well as asking if the sun fish might suddenly appear in the Firth of Forth, if the 1976 summer was hot enough for them to magically appear. Father was a former Professor of Sociology at Beijing University; he'd fled the Cultural Revolution in 1972, sensing clearly where China was heading. *Sun fish are found in every tropical sea. They eat jellyfish* is what Professor Ling-Wei said, so Gina kept her eyes peeled. At twelve, though, she'd totally rebelled.

"A large portion of chips with cod and pickles," said the well dressed Edinburgh lawyer at the end of a long rights filled day. He leaned on the counter, eager to talk and let off steam. He liked the elderly odd Chinese guy who owned this place; he's low key. Tie loosened, he's had it up to here with demanding relatives and oily deals. The only grease he can hack right now is in Ling-Wei's fish and chip shop on Portobello's sea front. Sticky intense July air had infected Edinburgh's heart, pushing some no doubt to over drive and stress in it all its toxic manifestations. Here by the sea people could take proper time to breathe and listen – if not to the actual sea then to themselves. The Professor had kept his academic title all these years he'd owned and run the shop ever since he'd escaped from the Red Guard guns and their thirsts for politico-socio purge.

"Hot day, huh? I'm just about to go and crash out on myself. Can't face telly right now, no noise thank you. Why are some people just never happy with what they have, hmm? Is this a western illness in the mind do you think?"

"I'm not sure about that. The search for contentment seems an endless universal game, doesn't it. People look for it in all kinds of places. Do you want soy on that, or any fry mushrooms?"

The sounds of frying onions and potatoes dominated the shop front. On the wall there's a calendar recording the moon's movements and various Chinese astrological interpretations. Professor Ling-Wei was born in 1944, the year of the monkey. He's shrewd enough not to alienate this good customer with an anti-western consumer tirade. Particularly now that China's economy and patterns of consumption have exploded, out classing the West. But being a deep thinking soul at heart, he thrills at serving up thought with relish. When the shop is quiet in the winter months and his academic translation work for the Scottish university dries up it gets very boring relying only upon www.chinadaily.com.cn for inspiring words.

"I think you are probably right about the game part. It's seems it's not fashionable sitting round the table thrashing out and negotiating out differences free of charge. I shouldn't really complain here, should I? Good lawyers make their living out of this when politicians simply cannot be bothered."

Professor Tommy Ling-Wei can tell that this bright lawyer is fishing and clearly wants to engage in some kind of ad-hoc debate-while-you-wait-to-eat. The chips will be another five minutes or so; he needed to fill the waiting time somehow. There's no piped musak in his shop as he couldn't hear himself think and quiet time these days seems an exotic and endangered luxury. His former wife and daughter live together in Beijing; Gina is a Director of a factory which makes plastic toys and shoes. He makes do with the rooms above his shop; it's enough to live in. He needs no more. It's enough to see the open space of the sea.

"I think we all need to climb out of our respective boxes sometimes, step out of what is known and familiar, take small risks. You seem pre-occupied with the day and if you don't mind me suggesting this – I don't make a habit of this, you know, as I know my place as well as my plaice by now. While you are waiting why don't you just pop out briefly and pick up some sea weed for me? This may sound incredible but you can use it in food like you can a lot of foods. Please try."

There was something in the humility and wisdom of this Chinese guy's tone – *it's not exactly an order from on high is it;* thinks the West End hot-shot lawyer who, like a lot of Britons is secretly ultra sensitive about status, buying power and being patronised. He'd been coming to this ordinary looking chippy for over a year now, having discovered it by accident after one particularly long drawn out tribunal. The guy had even put an empty cardboard fish and chip box on the counter for him to put the seaweed in. Bizarre, but he appears harmless. Why not just step out briefly to oblige him? Maybe it's some weird Chinese remedy, accoutrement, product placement even. Who knows? So off the lawyer trotted towards the shore with the power of suggestion. He'd heard that the Chinese ate chocolate ants, birds nests, cats – but sea weed was a first.

Gathering some up quickly and stuffing it in to the box; he walks back in to the shop. Glancing down at his plush designer suit, he sees some water has splashed a fair bit on his trousers. He'd not even noticed. No doubt in the high powered office he works in where there was no permanent escape from four walled politics, no doubt he'd get no end of comments and stick. Staff there were on the constant look out for one – up –man-ship, a joke at another's expense, signs of deviancy or delusions of grandeur. After all, it was the real price of conformity, wasn't it. A necessary degree of sacrificing your individuality and identity to fit in, be accepted, thought 'decent' and hard working. And a price he is prepared to pay and chooses to pay at the end of the day believing totally in the idea, practice, philosophy and rhetoric of free will.

The fish and chips are cooked to perfection. Smiling, the odd Chinese guy looks happy sliding the sea weed back towards him over the counter.

"There will be a use for it this, I think", the chip shop owner says, giving him his change due. It can be great – the things that turn up unexpectedly on the shore line of life. Anything frankly which will break the dull but sanctimonious routine. An extra gherkin's been thoughtfully squeezed in to the take away box, the lawyer notes, walking back to his car parked nearby. But what the point of the sea weed was, he'd never know. It is a mystery between him, the Chinese guy and the deep blue sea. Munching in to the gherkin inside the car, he doesn't really want to know reasons either, having forgotten about the day and the water on his suit. He'd been after cod, not God after all. Tomorrow and the day after that will more than provide enough angst and quagmire. After eating he drives off in to heavy traffic.

*

Professor Ling-Wei had discovered Buddhism quite late on in life; believing that this body of thought didn't appear to make great claims about any great leaps forward or indeed backwards. No, Buddhism was more about *inner* leaps of faith which could not really be marketed, as much as the markets might want this. And so much for that other Great Idea: the liberal idea of a linear line of 'progress' in the human condition or within society generally. He's not sure about that either, having seeing peasants being murdered and shot at and now seeing new subtle scapegoats here in the free West, both covert and overt purgings going on even here in the United Kingdom which always proclaimed itself a fair country. When he'd been teaching in Beijing in the late sixties and early seventies; he'd looked with genuine admiration at the UK seeing how humanely that Island mediated between state, corporate and individual.

But not now. Now what of the world with its global cheap supermarket of opinions? Every nation was caught up in this insane race to some imagined somewhere. Maybe ultimately there *was* no finishing line, ever. Earlier that day, after reading an email from his ex-wife who he's on speaking terms with, he'd read an online article about how academic researchers at South Taiwan university had discovered that sitting in brightly lit environments is more conducive to honest, ethical behaviour. It made him laugh out loud, like the good old days. The old days back when he was a young married man and the local chi doctor said his wife had too much wind and he not enough so that marital energies needed to be balanced constantly.

He had to watch his sense of humour though, here in Scotland. Not everybody appreciated too clever a pair of clogs, a smart intellectual or being subjected to exposure. He hankered hungrily after new Sociological theory, new papers to feed the intellect. It had been a challenge reigning in his enquiring mind. Reading the British papers out of curiosity, he's amazed to see how savage the attacks are on publicly funded schools and hospitals. *You want savage intrusive state then you should have lived through what I lived through*, he muttered to himself only the other day over lunch time noodles.

He'd thought about sending in an email to a local *Your Shout* newspaper column but declined. Better conserve your energy and sanity instead; do practical compassionate things when and how you can. The animal kingdom will appreciate it if not the realm of the human. And sometimes the thought would have to be enough; it was all he could afford. It's July and the university is on summer recess so he's out on a limb right now as one source of income has dried up. He'd kept his academic title. It's part of his identity, though he's had to diversify to survive. Most of his former colleagues in Beijing who he's kept in contact with have had to do the same. Chinese university salaries and pensions were not what they were once.

The friendly locals in Portobello who he's got to know over the years clearly thought he earnt a small fortune marking papers for the university and running a small shop. It amused him greatly, yet doesn't surprise him. The imagined bamboo always grew better and faster somewhere else for human kind. This was always true in China and the UK, no matter what type of state administration or government. A few regulars came in, ordering the usual and he noted the cool new breeze which the evening brought. If the weather was warm enough he may swim again in the sea, grateful for small simple pleasures. The forecast was good for the next days but then again, seeing was a kind of believing. But he *has* seen seals several times popping up their heads; dark limpid eyes watching the human goings on. The chatty lawyer, that fast young buck he'd served earlier hadn't realised the joke about the extra gherkin or the seaweed. Not every gift had a hidden catch; some things really just were after all. They just occur, as in nature. As his daughter Gina occurred and still occurs; she who refused to be labelled or controlled by either parent. She'd wrestled with Chinese society too. Like the rest of the world it had profoundly ambivalent feelings about powerful independent women. It was ever thus and always true.

The gherkin had helped that lawyer take his mind off the day's turmoil just for a small moment without him realising it. That and the seaweed. Recently the professor's been coughing up a lot of mucus; maybe it was the cheap instant coffee he drinks but he thought the seaweed might help cure the phlegm. Chinese medicine was wondrous in this way. And just for a moment that lawyer thought outside the chip box and suspended the stories we always tell ourselves about the place we occupy in the universe. There he'd been out on the sea shore picking up the damp green mass; a different kind of fish out of water. Tommy Ling-Wei finds Zen and picking up seaweed is great for this, this seeing over and though Great Walls both within and without – this thinking outside the habitual. He thought extra pickle might be an interesting humanitarian idea; a generous gesture with bite and attitude.

And he'd seen plenty of this sweet and sour posturing walking round Edinburgh streets right enough: young women particularly who happily read books whilst crossing busy roads and not giving a hoot whether they were run over or honked at just as long as the book is read. But he couldn't complain about his time in Edinburgh: he'd been anonymously accepted and not publicly questioned which had to be better than what he'd endured in China. His own daughter Gina had been single minded like that; about fighting for her right to call her identity and life her very own – even though this raised some people's hackles. Maybe tomorrow it might be misty again and he could stroll casually up to Arthur's Seat and take in the ambient vapours imagining he's once more in some steam filled rice field in the middle of nowhere.

Last week he'd had a walk about town; admiring the retro street lights set in pavements in Lothian Road outside the Standard Life Building and taking in the random yet sublime wit of delicate weeds growing out of drain grills in Princes Street. An elegant soiling of the aesthetic. Walking was always great to clear the mind. And last November some people created fantastical taper filled paper lanterns on Portobello Beach; releasing the glowing creations off like balloons in to the rich blue. He'd made a wish each time he saw a lantern; he'd said a silent mantra. Maybe they were souls looking for some kind of homeland. Other times he'd seen people playing violins on the beach; even a mini Bazaar of little tents. It was all curiously satisfying to see. The city had changed in some ways since 1972; yet some still asked where he *stayed* as oppose to where he *lived*. He was thrown at first by the term *the day* as opposed to *to-day;* but philosophically speaking, he'd been delighted by the local term 'the now' as the now and what it truly is had always been up for intellectual-definitional grabs. But he'd learnt fast and worked hard; adapting and learning the language. You had to, to survive. Locking up shop then and pulling down corrugated shutters; he entered the separate front door to his flat.

文化大革命

The day giant panda swim across Yangtze River is the day you condemn another

Forever In Blue Jeans

The white wedding cake had little pink roses on it. It was a multi tiered creation with three storeys and thick icing and it took Robert Muir, my da , and his assistant weeks to make it as they had to order the special marzipan decorations from down south in England, land of the Sassenachs. It was just after the war, so you couldn't get fancy stuff for cakes easily then. The rest they crafted themselves. Robert was sure his fiancée Angela would like it. Women were proving to be expensive, like grandfather cabbie Stewart Muir warned. Business at the Fountain Bridge bakery was bearing up; it was just as well the scotch pies and sausage rolls were proving a hit with the lads at the brewery. Workers came in at lunchtime, bringing the smog in with them as they entered. All that was before I was born. My name at birth was Shirley Muir and I was born in 1954 in a small flat above the bakery. I followed my grandpa's line of work, but I went one better as now I own my own private hire cab firm. It is called *Shirley's Wheels* and it holds its own against the big boys. I will tell you more about this if you can bear with me. My memory and concentration is not what it used to be, I think it is the effect of the drugs. God almighty, if only I can remember straight. I was too wee to remember seeing Sean Connery doing milk rounds nearby.

As a girl I was told the story of how ma met da so many times it bored me. Grandpa Stewart seems to wheel the story out each Christmas, along with the ragged looking Christmas tree. My mum Angela had been working as a secretary at the brewery and dad had noticed her red hair when she had come in to the bakery to buy some rolls. They courted for over two years and Grandpa Stewart Muir the black cab driver had hinted at a wedding. Stewart had hoped that his only son Robert would also become a black cab driver when he returned from fighting in Europe. After all, the money was good as a cabbie, enough to cushion the effects of rationing. But da was having none of it. "The future is in pies and bread. People always need those," he said. Angela made her wedding dress herself to save shillings. They moved in to the small flat above the bakery and Angela started work in the shop, serving customers and doing accounts.

*

Da's face is red and warm looking from the oven out the back. He has been baking bread since five in the morning. The bakery has a small yard area where wooden crates are stacked and there is a tiny area for plants and a wooden shed. His disappointment is visible. The workers still come in at lunch time from the brewery but the smog has gone now. I am fourteen and I have just cut my hair very pixie short. They, the parents, the God Almighty's, want me to stay on at college to learn some typing skills. The other God Almighty's, the teachers at school – they have decided that I am not clever enough for what they call the eleven plus. Now God help *me*, I have realised I am what they call 'working class'. I heard the term on a posh television programme ma was watching as she patches a quilt up. I pretend not to notice as ma pins and tucks, sighing.

"Can you do anything right at all, do you think? And what about that bloody awful hair? I do hope you are not turning in to one of those hippies. I heard all about them. Free love? Is that what it's called? I call it dirty minds."

My mind and body freeze at this latest attack. I can't think of a quick thing to fire back at her so I sit very still. I thought she'd be pleased at my hair. She said she always wanted a boy anyway. I am bored as I sit and watch her patch. The big clock stroke radio come TV wooden thing dominates the room. It is ugly and I don't like it. It frightens me for some reason. I don't care how long the God Almighty's had to save every week to buy it. I turn and flee from this stifling room with the tick tick tick and the click click click. I'm off to a night club down Leith Walk where I can get in if I'm wearing enough make up. My wee powder compact and mirror shows big black fraught deer eyes if you look close enough. Thing is, most people don't see that well.

My knowledge of the darkness began when I was five or six I think. Don't know exactly. I remember having a terrible repeating dream about a witch woman staring at me through the open letter box as I was sitting at the top of the stairs which led down to the bakery. I used to sit in the gloom at the top of the stairs playing with dolls and waiting for them to finish the shifts at the bakery. Every now and then a sweet waft of warm dough drifts up the stairs to the flat. Later, I chop the doll's golden hair off as her too perfect face looks smug. I couldn't really tell anyone about the dream as the God Almighty's were either too busy or tired or thought I was being silly. I learnt about witches and dark things from the book I borrowed from the school library. Then I realised the dark things exist *in the grown ups too* and not just in the woods, as I saw the punches and the looks my ma gives my pa when she discovers he has been looking at those magazines full of naked women. She beats him black and blue, but he carries on buying the magazines anyway – I saw them filed away in secret places. I switch off under the hand knitted patchwork blankets when I hear the thuds, the cries, the smashed plates and screams. At night, I see and try to confront the witch who wants to put me in an oven but the smell of warm golden pies always defers this horror…

*

Forever In Blue Jeans is a hit song by Neil Diamond and I really like listening to it on the car radio. I am driving my yellow Ford Cortina to my caravan which is parked in a site in Granton, near the sea. A lot of canny folk say Granton is ugly. There is a big gas works there, but I like it because you can be sure nobody will want to go there. It has been a busy day; I must have driven around Edinburgh several times. I have got a really good young lass who takes the calls from the punters and radios them over to me and the other two drivers. It is only a small office near Gorgie Road, but it is all my own. In the hot summer of 1976 da ran off with a rich Australian woman, which drove ma to booze. The outback must have swallowed them up. But guess who has to attend to ma often in police cells and hospital wards? Sometimes, a person can be in a kind of private jail in the mind and yet be free to move around like other outsiders.

I just like blue jeans, that's all there is to it. I wish I was a teenager again just driving around bonny Edinburgh. I was carefree then; listening to Neil Diamond's greatest. I just like blue jeans, they are forever me. As I say, most folk can't see the hidden *emotional violence* that goes on. I must admit, I nicked that phrase from my doctor. The medication helps me forget parents and pasts and control my anger. I started on dope but migrated right enough.

Maybe just a pipe dream, but perhaps I'm just a throw back longing for my leathers, jeans and cow-boy boots. Those were the glory years, the 70s and 80s. Recession? *What recession?* I was having a right old laugh. If I see any more politicians on TV ranting on about jobs and taking personal responsibility I'll crack again. But I will never mention the bloke I topped off. No. Nobody will ever know about *that* ultimate teenage act of rebellion. I was only fourteen and wearing my favourite denims as he drove me away from said nightclub down Leith Walk. My Audrey Hepburn doe eyes didn't realise what a wolf he was until he started to fumble at my zip. I cut him with my nail file. Events and the God Almightys pushed me over some edge then. Some secrets we carry to the grave.

French Evolution

Jacques and Isabel Borel live contentedly enough near the famous Gobelin tapestry factory-museum in Paris's thirteenth arrondissement. A childless couple in their fifties, Monsieur Borel works part time as a guide and security man in the factory-museum but in younger years had made tapestries himself. His wife did occasional embroidery, took in alterations and lined curtains and coats on an ancient sewing machine that took pride of place in their flat. They reside in a rather magnificent block of 'social housing' flats built around 1900. The concierge, Monsieur Arteuil, encourages high standards of hygiene in the block and in the summer the fancy green wrought iron balconies host a flowery riot of reds, oranges and pinks with geraniums, small roses, nasturtiums.

The couple live modestly enough on the fourth floor, sharing with three other flats. They keep their four rooms (including a small bathroom) and balcony to high standards of cleanliness. The grooved shutters are dusted regularly. They had been careful with money throughout their thirty year marriage. Isabel excels at the art of finding fresh good quality vegetables at low prices – in lean times scouring streets after market stalls had finished trading to gather slightly bruised looking but perfectly edible produce. She has a fiery but principled personality and doesn't care what people think about the way this scrabbling around in the gutter looked. This feisty spirit attracted Jacques initially – as well as her fine upstanding frame and bones. Pleasures included cinema and maybe a glass of cognac or a cigarette while listening to the radio. She dyes her hair a chestnut brown and doesn't mind if grey roots reappear. If Isabel is the eccentric, spontaneous liberal half of the marriage then Jacques is the formal, ordered and officious conservative. His sense of order and habit is so ingrained that he has fought for years for his 'right' to sleep on the right hand side of the marital bed – the side which faced the window and got the first few narrow stripes of morning light. These sleeping arrangements were a great battle ground for power: there were times when Isabel had threatened to withhold sex if she too did not get a chance to sleep facing the shutters and the light. She used guerrilla tactics and had refused to wash his clothes or cook food. These ruses worked and after furious exchanges Jacques would be forced to relent and then sulked behind a copy of *Le Monde*. They avoided discussion of political or religious matters, then, as each would not budge an inch. Eventually things calmed down and a mutual tolerance ensued. It is a marriage of opposites but in truth each would be bored with a compliant or docile partner.

The flats are elegant but solid and almost form a square, but for the two high black gates and railings that lead to the housing enclosure. The heavy gates are open to anyone – there is no entry phone system or hidden camera. Anybody can walk in off the street to visit a resident. Early every morning the concierge pries a gate open and weighs it down with a rock so workers can go off to work and parents can walk their children to school without the gates constantly clanging and creaking, which annoys the housebound elderly and retired people who also live in the block. Once a week fresh groceries, milk and sometimes wine is left in a wooden grocery box in a foyer for the concierge to deliver to those residents who are too old, frail or sick to go shopping for themselves.

And it is through these gates, at precisely seven in the morning, that Monsieur Borel makes his way after shaving and descending down from the flat – beginning his walk to work. His punctuality, reliability and squeaky highly polished patent shoes arc legendary in the Gobelins, where he has worked for twenty odd years. He stops briefly to speak and joke with his old friend the newspaper vendor, who has a kiosk near Les Gobelins metro station. He cuts a dapper figure with his official suit and badge, combed slicked back hair and trim moustache. He is slightly plumper than he was fifteen years ago – but overall he has managed to retain his physique. It is late March and there are a few tourist group bookings for this afternoon. He sees them neatly entered in the visitor book. He is in the small office near the grand columned entrance created by Formige in 1913, with its exterior 'gallery' facade of tapestry making figures and instruments depicted in decorative stone circles. It looks like it might rain. He had a bad accident with one of his thumbs about ten years ago. It got caught in a loom and so he had to forfeit his job as *lissier,* or hand weaver, and be content instead with guiding curious and sometimes demanding tourists around in French and basic English. The working factory was re-opened to the public in 2003 – after the state finally decided that it was worth pouring public money in to. It is another ordinary morning. After his coffee he attends to various administrative duties – not least of which involve answering emails and letters of enquiry and interest about the tapestries.

Once weavers and spinners for French kings and nobility and royalty across Europe, Gobelins now wove for state commissions and diplomacy. Today there are thirty five lissiers working on commissions – sometimes working through the night at short notice. Until this point everything has been predictable, Jacques has eaten breakfast, complained to Isabel again about the piles of laundry and unfinished alterations lying about in the living room and had a mildly amusing chat with his friend at the newspaper kiosk. But the letter that he now holds in his hand (internal mail from his line manager) is unusual: an ominous sign? With trembling hands he reads that he is to have an informal interview tomorrow morning with Simon Lourdet, his Manager, regarding a possible three month exchange placement abroad.

So it is with a somewhat preoccupied expression that Jacques Borel walks back home later that afternoon. He makes his way slowly down the Avenue des Gobelins towards the large roundabout. The dark grey clouds which hung so threateningly in the sky earlier that day now yield dark grey heavy rain. He unfurls a large umbrella. Water runs down roofs, bounces off passing cars, drips off shop fronts, shakes leaves on trees. His shoes seem to squeak more than usual. But this is of no matter, he reflects. What are two shoes in the face of such a development? His shoes will last. Two incredibly irritating German tourists tested his patience to the limit earlier with their questioning of his limited English and their claims that in the seventeenth century German tapestries were every bit as fine as French ones.

He is due to see Monsieur Lourdet at nine thirty. *A possible exchange placement abroad at his age!* He has heard of such exchanges before but thought that they were limited to academic placements and research. He has only been abroad twice in his life. As a teenager he flew with his family for a week to stay in London. He despised the food there but loved the big parks. As a newly married couple he and Isabel went for a few days to Switzerland. *Don't get too carried away*, he tells himself turning in to Boulevard Vincent Auriel.

*

Isabel is smoking a cigarette by the fireplace as he comes in. She's been busily machining her way through virtually all the alterations in the room. Taking off his wet coat, Jacques sees piles of neatly folded and ironed clothes in the half gloom ready to be returned to owners for payment. About time. He sometimes feels he lives in a laundry.

"Look at the state of you! Here is a towel. Did you wipe your shoes on the mat? I hope so, I washed the hall floor too." She throws a towel at him. He grunts a response to her. He is tired and needs an hour or so of quiet.

"Well, I see you are in a fine mood. Don't mind me. There's fresh fish and bread. Maybe you ought to lie down. You look a little pale. Nobody robbed you today, eh?"

"No, nobody." He goes through to the bedroom to lie down, shutting the door behind him. Isabel's mother never mentioned that marriage was another kind of work, requiring an athlete's stamina and a politician's eye for an opportunity. Sensitivity is sometimes needed and an ability to listen – but only when the other party deserved a listening ear. *Give too much and they take a mile*, her mother said – and this was true of relations at work with one's boss and true within love.

Over supper Jacques cautiously mentions the letter. He watches his wife's face carefully, not sure how she will respond to the idea of his possible absence for three months. But Isabel seems calm and interested – adding coolly that if his pay arrangements were to remain then she could deal with the rent. He is secretly disappointed that she did not say she would miss him. Later, he cannot sleep so he steals in to the kitchen and pours himself wine. It is quiet apart from the occasional car and clacking of heels on the pavements outside.

*

Monsieur Simon Lourdet sits in his own designated office at the back of the museum building. Tasteful prints of Paris and the tapestries hang on walls. He has always liked Jacques Borel's attitude to work: punctuality, honesty, smart appearance. Customers and clients, as well as visitors had commented on him – on the way he efficiently yet thoroughly responded to enquiries and demands. So when this opportunity had arisen for a staff member to be posted abroad for three months he had steered away from selecting an archivist or even one of the weavers – but instead thought of the ex-weaver who so loyally delivered good customer service and reception. Lourdet knows that it is often the reception and the service which are the most memorable aspects of visitor experience. He smiles at Jacques, who comes in apprehensively. He gets straight to the point, explaining that he wants to officially nominate Jacques on a European funded state museum exchange programme which involves choosing a UK state museum as the host countries are rotated.

All Jacques's expenses – the cost of the flight, his accommodation and living expenses are to be paid for – and in case he is worried about his rent here he would continue to have his wage paid in to his account so his wife could still access funds to pay the rent. It will be an opportunity to thank Jacques for his hard work – it might also be a working holiday as well as a chance to develop his skills and practice his English. His role abroad will be ushering and guiding visitors, translating for French visitors. He can use canteen facilities and will have expenses too. Lourdet is looking for

Jacques to fly out in the next ten days and all that he needs is his agreement and a signature from him. There is silence as Monsieur Lourdet waits patiently.

"Where exactly in the UK will I be stationed?" stammers Jacques.

"You have a choice of three cities according to the documentation: Manchester, Cardiff or Edinburgh. London is off the list, I'm afraid, as it is too popular."

Jacques has always been curious about Scotland – it seems to him that the people were like the landscape: hardy, a bit wild sometimes, rugged and uncompromising. Yet also melancholic and quietly emotional. It is Edinburgh that he chooses and promptly signs along the form.

Jacques is struck by the National Museum of Scotland's exterior and the way the old is combined with the new. Walking up the steps with his two heavy bags, he notices little hedges and plants on the rounded concrete roof-tower's roof. He likes the elegance with which April bulbs had been laid out in Princes Street Gardens. The black railings reminded him of Paris. He suddenly feels shy. Is his English good enough? He knows that Scottish people are different from English people so he has to be sensitive about lumping British characteristics together. People from different regions of France felt the same way. In fact there is a big debate about it now in politics back home: issues of identity, food, culture, loyalty to different levels of government. He hopes he won't offend anyone. Travelling in to central Edinburgh was straightforward and people told him where to disembark. A little girl on the bus seemed fascinated by his moustache so he smiled quickly and then looked away. He is shown to the human resources department and is greeted warmly by Mary McTavish, a short blond woman in a white shirt and tartan waistcoat.

"You had a good flight? You begin on Monday so you have the weekend to settle in, maybe take a tour around Edinburgh and sort yourself out. I will be your manager for the next three months, so if you have any problems or questions please do come and talk to me. You have a locker, swipe card and key like everyone else and your uniform will be available on Monday. Sorry, am I speaking too fast?"

"Non. No. It is alright, I can understand you." Jacques mutters before she starts again.

"I will give you a lift to your accommodation which is not far from here – we just go along Nicholson Street. This is e side of Edinburgh, very cosmopolitan. Your designated flat was occupied by a curator but has been empty for the last three months: it might need a bit of a re-clean, apologies."

*

Number Six Oxford Street has a decent white front door but Jacques can see that nobody has lived there for a while. Mary shows him inside, apologising for the dust and offering to buy some groceries in the same breath. She promptly darts away only to return with fresh bread, some oven meals, milk, juice and apples. She leaves a map, hand drawn directions to the museum, some keys and guide book.

"That's it, then." She smiles. "There's a microwave, radio and working fridge so you'll get your bearings. No washing machine unfortunately but a good launderette nearby. Anything you want to ask me? Well then, good night. I expect you will want a rest."

The tenement flat is on the ground floor with cream painted walls and high ceilings. It overlooks the street. A small patch of grass with a washing line is at the back. Jacques has never slept away from his wife since they were married – he almost feels bereaved or that some part of his body was missing. He notices that clean sheets, pillowcase and blanket have been placed on a bed in the bedroom at the back. A huge mirror hangs on the wall opposite the bed: he catches himself yawning. Maybe the previous occupier, the curator, had a secret kinky love life and watched his carnal adventures in mirrors. With the British all the passion is underground and comes out in strange ways. After a snack supper he lies in the bed staring at the ceiling mouldings, which resemble fruit, before finally falling asleep.

*

Jacques soon adjusts to work. His first few days are strange but his colleagues are welcoming. Mary McTavish is known as "The Clinch" (he has trouble pronouncing this) amongst staff as she has an eagle eye for absences, punctuality and performance. Hamish Pringle is another visitor guide and shows him the daily routine: locker room, canteen, how to sign in as well as showing him round the vast museum. He particularly likes the live fish in the stylish entrance hall. On Tuesday he calls Isabel from the HR office phone. She is well, it has rained a lot in Paris and Monsieur Arteuil the concierge was greasing the gates himself as there are complaints about noise again. Poor old Madame Savoir on the top floor of the opposite block has had a sudden heart attack and died. But some are saying she choked on a chicken bone, which served her right for always insisting on white meat. There was a commotion and two ambulance men carried her body out discreetly under white sheets. Nobody knows if she has any relatives, as she had no visitors so Monsieur Arteuil is having to wait a decent enough time before clearing possessions. So that is that .*C'est fin*.

Gradually Jacques explores Edinburgh, enjoying much of what he sees, although he is bemused by the constant *rush* people seem to be in. Nobody seems to stroll along. It is as if the collective is caught up in one big mind rush, nobody really sits on the benches in the public spaces just for the sheer pleasure. There has to be a reason for everything, a justification for remaining immobile. He admires views from the castle battlements. Travelling down to Leith one day he sees an enormous Buddha like Rastafarian tramp sitting between two huge bags of belongings. The tramp smiles enigmatically or stares blankly in to space. Perhaps stillness is feared, Jacques thinks, because of the possible madness or emptiness that might follow. He has never seen so many public bars before or such hedonism in the extra long limousines driving about with screaming and waving girls inside. He waves back – not sure if this is customary. Is this another side to Scottish sober reserve? But he likes the Botanic Gardens and the little sentimental statue of the Grey Haired Friar's Bobby.

In early May Isabel sends a letter telling Jacques that Monsieur Arteuil has now successfully cleared poor old Madame Savoir's flat only to now discover that she apparently had a long lost cousin from the south who was most irate about the selling off of the apartment possessions. Unfortunately there was no will or legal document left. Isabel has a wedding dress to alter, which is keeping her busy. Jacques has become quite fond of his little home, but to curb his occasional homesickness he manages to tune the radio to French World Service programmes. Hamish tells him that there is a 'work night-out' soon which entails drinks in George Street followed by a traditional ceilidh dance.

"Don't worry, you don't have to do the dancing if you would rather not," Hamish says over one lunch break. "But if you want me to show you some basic steps, just say. It will give you an idea about traditional Scottish culture and all that".

*

The pub is crammed with office workers recovering from the week. Large salon mirrors adorn walls and the building's former identity as a bank is revealed by a now redundant but ornate safe mechanism in one wall. Elaborate mouldings on the high ceilings show scrolls painted in gold and green. People sit chatting around tables eating hot food on a raised platform. Jacques turns around, feeling Hamish tap on his shoulder. It is early in the evening but already there are rowdy elements gathering round a big flat screen showing football in bright lurid colours.

"We are all over here, Jacques! Don't get lost in the crowd."

Jacques follows Hamish to a corner where about twenty Museum staff are gathered. He squeezes himself down next to a young woman, trying to make sure he does not spill his tonic water over her. He drank some wine earlier, but does not want to get completely drunk. Even on social occasions his innate reserve and sense of propriety is pronounced.

"Who are you, then? Don't think I've met you before pal." She has bright blue eye shadow and blonde hair. She has drunk quite a bit already; Jacques can smell it on her along with a very strong perfume. He tenses slightly, feeling awkward.

"I'm Suzi Lugg, work in administration – I do typing and stuff. I work up on the fifth floor hidden away from folk. What is it that you do?"

Jacques explains that he is a temporary visitor guide from Paris on an exchange programme. Suzi giggles and asks Jacques if he is a romantic Frenchman. He replies rather formally that he is married and that he and his wife celebrate wedding anniversaries every year. Making an excuse to go the men's room, he sweats on the way downstairs to the dark toilets. Once upstairs again he discovers that the crowd has moved to another room which has been kitted out with live musicians and dancing. Hamish is dancing with a woman to fiddle music and it is not long before Suzi is suggestively catching his eye. In a kind of polite desperation he leaves.

*

Later that night he is again restless and cannot sleep. He catches himself staring off in to the darkened room. Troubling thoughts arise in the corners of his mind. Maybe he is getting the mad tramp disease, or the British air is affecting him. He misses the feel of Isabel at night and the easy chats with the weavers. The girl's words at the pub affected him deeply. For the first time in years, Jacques Borel doubts himself. Why be disturbed by a young woman who did not really know him? And yet he had a secret fear that he was *not* a spontaneous romantic, but instead a boring, predictable officious type. He realises he does not have much fun. As for the Rastafarian tramp he'd seen: well, was Jacques's own response any better? It's easy to criticise others, but maybe the man had fallen on hard times or had been in a mental institution. It is not so much a question of fear or judgement. He realises with a shock that *he* did not have much compassion, empathy or even curiosity for the tramp. In some way he feels incomplete, stale. Okay, his life is ordered and stable and 'decent' – yet he senses there was much beyond his own thoughts and world view, so many other experiences to be tasted.

These unsettling feelings remain when waking the next Saturday morning. Walking along Nicholson Street with a slight hangover to the launderette he has discovered nearby, he is suddenly startled by the sight of two tiny yellow and pale blue birds fluttering and rolling about together on the pavement.

"Just bluetits mating, I think." A passing woman comments as she sees Jacques's astonishment. The wild violence in love! He notices that he is standing in front of an antique junk shop. On a sudden whim, he walks in – somehow compelled to look around. Still carrying his dirty laundry, he peers around the dusty gloom of the junk shop. The shop goes back a long way, there are piles of stuff everywhere: clothes, plates, furniture, clocks, books, shoes, jewellery. Two carved plaster faces catch his eye: they look like copies or casts of some medieval stone faces found in churches. One face looks stern and frowns, the other face looks neutral and calm. They are obviously male and have pointed peasant looking hats. He buys them and places them on a chest of drawers back at the flat. He is sure he has seen something like them before, but he can't remember where. Perhaps he will look in the museum's archives.

Isabel has never experienced anything like this before. She wonders for a moment if she is losing her sanity. Lying back on the bed, she keeps her eyes shut. Light filters through the shutters: it is late May, leaves are out and Paris looked and felt re-newed. But there they are again in her mind's eye: an endless stream of puffy white clouds appearing and floating by on some distant but infinite horizon. It has happened every morning for about a week – this sensation of watching clouds when her eyes were shut. She gazes at an old framed black and white photograph of her mother on a chest of drawers. These last few weeks she has realised she misses Jacques. It has been a struggle to admit it.

The Madame Savoir drama is now over. Isabel has been lonely. She goes in to Gobelins Museum to speak briefly to the weavers and have a chat. Over coffee she laughs and mentions the arguments over who slept where in the marital bed – but it feels strange to have no husband to nag, wash clothes for, eat with or make love to. Perhaps she is not a good wife, she laments to herself as she buys fresh vegetables from *Tang Frères* on Avenue de Choisy – the biggest Chinese grocery in Paris. The thirteenth arrondissement has a mixture of old housing. La Petite Asie is situated here too which means that it is possible to overhear Cantonese and Vietnamese conversations while haggling over prices. In the 1980s, ethnic Chinese refugees from the former French colony of Indochina arrived – much to the resentment of some Parisians. After delivering the alterations she has been working on, Isabel finds herself wandering in to the Francois Mitterrand library. She is transfixed by stone images of virgin and child in a book she finds on religious iconography. She is amazed when she sees it is closing time. She has been there for hours. Slowly, she walks home.

*

Electricity builds steadily in the dense clouds above the streets around Jacques's tenement block. Trees sway in a pre-storm build up and down on these streets people glance up knowingly and hurry home with shopping and brief cases. Jacques sits at the small table in the kitchen eating some lunch, listening to the growing rumblings high in the sky as if someone is moving a huge grand piano around. For some odd reason the two carved stone faces that he bought from the antique shop in South Clerk Street unnerved him – he has put them outside by the washing line posts on the shared drying green whilst he makes up his mind up what to do with them. It was the thought of these two staring faces stuck forever in perpetual expressions that freaked him out one night so he had put them out. Whilst rummaging around outside finding a suitable place for them, he thought he heard a faint meow but he can't be sure. Rain arrives, with intense flashes of lightening casting strange, freakish webs of white light in the darkened sky.

He happens to look up and suddenly, to his utter astonishment, he sees a blue coiled light suspended right in the middle of the kitchen. *Extraordinaire!* A perfect coiled spiral illuminated in bright blue. No sooner has he blinked than it has disappeared. What on earth has he seen? He wonders if his eyes are playing tricks on him. In France, he heard bizarre stories about electricity – stories of dogs, cows, and farmers struck dead by lightening. Rumblings outside grow louder and then there is a series of enormous cracks – Jacques realises that lightening has struck very close by. Rushing to the bedroom which looks out on the shared drying green he is just in time to witness a huge terrifying white finger of light pointing and flashing right down on to the ground. The whole garden area is bathed momentarily in an unnatural brightness. The next morning, in the damp dripping garden, Jacques is amazed and unnerved to see that the two stone faces have merged to form just a single smiling face.

*

Isabel starts to visit church again on Sunday mornings, as she did when she was a young girl with her mother. It is not far on the metro and she feels the services filled her in some way. She likes herself better after hearing about the trials and tribulations of those people in ancient times. Once, after hearing a service and request for donations and goods for a fund-raising event she decides to offer up her knitting so she sits and knits a figurine of sacred mother and child.

Jacques makes friends with a white male cat who he had heard scratching at the back door. He named him Bonaparte, but can't discover who he belonged to. Soon, Bonaparte becomes a trusted stamp and milk licker and regular companion. Work continues at the Museum and Jacques discovers that the two stone faces he bought from the antique shop were in fact copies from originals found in Notre Dame, Our Lady. When he finally leaves the National Museum at the end of June he is presented with a pink cake and a photograph of Edinburgh Castle. Suzi Lugg has kissed the card with bright pink lipstick. He takes a bus down to Leith and presents the black Rastafarian tramp with a piece of cake. Unsurprised, the tramp smiles mysteriously and begins to eat. Were people that still and un-self conscious touched by some divine force, some electricity – a bit like the grass and the stone faces being struck and touched by the lightening? Jacques knows it is a fine line between genius, mystic prophet and madman. He is just not sure anymore who makes that deciding defining line. He feels different now, as if some heavy gate in his mind has been opened.

Back in Paris, Monsieur Lourdet has collaborated with the *lissiers* to have a small tapestry panel spun for the hard working Borels. It shows a married couple in a bed, the husband on the left side and the wife on the right side against a flowery pastoral background. On the tapestry there is a small inscription: *someday change will be accepted as life itself.*

Lot Errata

A whole day hangs invariably on the hammer. The hammer dictates whether valuable flows of credit appear or not. And it definitely affects Scott Vigour's moods – no question. The hammer, that is. His livelihood after all. Some days it is touch and go – there are no guarantees that property will achieve the price it is assigned to. No, Scott instead uses guesstimates and the guesstimates are pretty accurate; that's why he's got a good reputation. Sitting in the mid eighteenth century townhouse-office in Great King Street Edinburgh; he glances wistfully at Esmeralda – an overfed but much loved gold fish who has been his companion for years. Esmeralda had been a consolation prize after the bitter divorce from Jetta, who still harangues him for casual sex from her des res pad in Peebles – despite the divorce.

They met at art school in London; she was the arty one – he the beatnik History of Art student – the critic who critiqued because he couldn't create – or so Jetta said. Jetta is turbo driven, a high flying bird who has an online lingerie business. They had fought bitterly, the divorce papers had come through – yet now both say they are merely separated to polite society and to anybody who should ask. Scott doesn't relish being on TV. Give me blessed anonymity, he mutters to himself, tapping in the results from yesterday's auction in Glasgow on to the company website. Yet he's to present another instalment of *What's My Home Worth?* tomorrow afternoon in Dalkeith. It's lunch time and he had grabbed a super strong coffee and a sarnie from Been Seen round the corner, nearly slipping on icy pavements. Philip, his surveyor colleague, is out viewing property. "It's just you and me, Esmé against the world," Scott whispers to his beloved fish, scattering some crumbs in to the tank and loosening his claret coloured tie.

*

The bare winter trees look elegant from a distance, like intricate lace fans. So much space between there and here, Christine Menelaws thinks, staring out of the sitting room window. Lately she has been catching herself staring in to space a lot – ever since he, the former ex- had weirdly and suddenly materialised out of nearby woods one misty afternoon. And this after a seven year disappearance during which nobody knew whether he had died, been murdered, emigrated. An unwanted ghost from the past; former police man Garry Menelaws had disappeared without trace. No paper trails, no blood or hair – no financial trails either. But there he had been standing – muddy, wet, unshaven and like a man possessed in her Dalkeith front room only three months ago.

And on top of this awful strange fact is the fact that her mother had only died in September and there are discrepancies in her will. Gaps in the narrative of her life that needed to be sorted before there can be any fair sharing of her estate. It had been a quiet London death and she and Alan had gone the distance to pay their respects. Brother Alan, a fork lift truck driver who lives in Greenock, has been helping his sister with the mortgage for the last few years. He knew there had been difficulties in his younger sister's marriage but this disappearance and now re-appearance had shocked him profoundly too. And Garry's surreal visit – out of the blue – it seemed both an eternity ago yet somehow only yesterday.

She had cried with the shock of it, but the rage came later. Christmas had been both farce and nightmare; it was a question of limping through social niceties at her brother's. For seven long years she had tried to come to terms with Garry's absence, his strange out of character disappearance. His former Lothian & Borders Police colleagues were at a loss; his oppressive Presbyterian mother was at a loss. The world was at a loss after thorough investigations – yet now she is the only one still feeling the pain of the lost seven years.

Garry had been remorseful, it was true – but there was something shifty and secretive in his manner. She offered him a glass of wine but had turned down his offer of sex. No, that was just too bloody weird. So the last three months had been crazy disorientated ones; her lifeguard colleagues at the swimming pool noticed her long silences.

And Garry hadn't told her the whole story. She now discovered he is living with a young blonde girl in a small house nearby. She had even seen them both in Dalkeith High Street, walking happily along without a care in the world – a real slap in the face. She had to manoeuvre out of sight to avoid the excruciating pain and embarrassment. *What on earth is he doing? Is he trying to humiliate me further?* She recalled that strange conversation with him in the front room again and again.

She had tried not to aggressively probe but she had to know where the hell he had been. The expression of anger – of violence even had always been forbidden in her family – yet the wine couldn't dissolve away the rage she felt as she had stared in to his apparently oblivious eyes, looking for answers, explanations. He spent some time in England, he said. In Worcester, with relatives to be precise. He just couldn't cope with the pressures of work and life and turning fifty.

It had been a really horrendous murder of a little girl by a paedophile which finally pushed him over the edge. He felt guilty as he let the culprit go, falling for his plausible manner. Couldn't live with himself then, he said. *But what the hell do you think it's been like living with your absence for the last seven years you selfish bastard,* she felt like screaming at him. Now seeing him with this young girl was the last straw. Christine had decided then to sell up and move away from the area completely. Dalkeith had done its time; she has to move away from where they had spent much of their married life. She'd go and live with her brother, she always liked the sea. She'd reclaim her long lost maiden name then and live the rest of her life as a Scott, though she was born in London. She stares at the open bottle of wine on the front room table. There's been too much booze and not enough food recently.

Television cameras are cumbersome things – like vast metallic creatures with eyes. Dead and dying brown leaves leave delicate imprints in ice that covers the ground. Scott shudders, wrapping his thick coat around him. Filming is nearly over, thank Christ for that. His nuts feel like they could drop off any minute. The house they are filming is a solid late nineteenth century number with good original features. He should have no problem shifting it, it's off a main road and there's a small garden too.

A woman had called the office yesterday requesting a visit and an initial evaluation – she said she also lived in Dalkeith which is very convenient. He will stop off and visit her with colleague Philip after filming is over. He throws a hungry crow the remains of a sandwich he bought at a filling station on the way. It looks suspiciously at the sandwich at first but then makes a lunge and flies off towards some trees. He had heard once that crows are actually incredibly intelligent and can use metal hooks to retrieve things from jars.

"Okay, Dave. Ready for action. Scott, sorry to be a pest but can we do that last section again – where you talk about the door? We missed the background. If you can just walk up the path again towards us doing the door bit."

Alex, the young director of *What's My Home Worth?* always wears a beret no matter what the weather. Sighing, Scott complies. Shouldn't really complain. Since he started presenting the show, business had boomed – so much so that the website was taking hundreds of hits per day. "That's when the website *is* actually working okay – Mr. Hyper Tense-Mark Up Man"; Philip joked recently. He is a large strapping man from Glasgow who knows how to cut good deals at the margins. And in the margins and away from the limelight is where Philip prefers to be, fortunately or unfortunately for Scott. So at least they are not rivals in that regard.

Philip winks at him from the side lines, enjoying Scott's obvious annoyance at filming a third take in semi arctic conditions. "Them there clouds up above laddy – them be snow clouds, I'm sure of it," says Philip, a bit of a wind up merchant though a low key one on the margins as stated. He points up towards the heavens, a pinky wash colour but with threatening clouds on the horizon. They probably have another two hours of daylight to view and evaluate the new client's property. Scott forces a sarcastic grin back at him. *Thank crunchie it's Friday,* he thinks as the cameras roll once more. Jetta always said that those types of clouds are called cumulus.

*

The doorknob might tell a few tales if only objects could talk. Christine Menelaws looks at the shiny silver doorknob on her bedroom door and catches a warped glance of herself in it. At fifty three, what man would want or desire her? Maybe someone out there will appreciate her somehow. Terrible aching emptiness eats away at her – what on earth will she do now with herself? As far as she knows there isn't a self help book available called "*How to re-build your whole life and self esteem once it has been decimated*" and she suspects that her grey hair roots have sprung up yet again. It seems only recently that she'd had her hair done again. At the pool earlier, she had seen a lady swimmer who was wearing a turquoise crucifix. Then she started thinking that maybe it really is the colour of God. And God knows she questioned the existence of God right now as she tries to make sense of the anguish, the lost years and betrayals. It has been a pig of a year.

She hadn't seen Garry again since that last time she saw him with his new lady *friend* as certain shop keepers in Dalkeith – ones who had run family businesses for years had archly described it. *Lady friend*. Emphasis was placed on both words with deadly and significant precision. It makes her more desperate to plan her escape from idle vicious tongues. If escape is ever really possible that is. Death's a kind of escape of course she thinks bitterly – and it felt terrible but she resents the fact that her mother had died. There were things she wanted to say to her. She slept badly last night, anxious about the surveyors visit today. The man from the Edinburgh estate agents and auctioneers sounded very assured and quite posh on the phone. But it is all a bit intimidating and then there had been the semi frantic cleaning of the house after she had finished her afternoon shift: toilet cleaned and any unpleasant dust and grease eliminated. A small room upstairs full of junk can easily double up as another bedroom; she wants to sell the property as a two bedroomed house. Her gaze at the packing cases and cardboard boxes is interrupted by a ring at the door.

"Mrs. Menelaws?" Scott Vigour gingerly holds out a hand for Christine to shake. Philip stands closely behind him beaming an encouraging smile. She's probably a recent widow or lonely single gran, he thinks. First time seller so be gentle with her. No rough house deals. Icy rain starts to fall behind the two men then as they step inside the modest hallway distributing some ice with them on to the hall carpet.

Scott unzips his briefcase, having already taken in the sea of boxes and cases that crowd out Christine's front room. The poor woman looks somehow lost in her belongings. There must have been a substantial sofa by the front bay window once, Philip notes, plonking himself on a black leather armchair and taking out his pad and tape measure. Now it is just bare space. Oddly disorientating. Christine nervously offers them tea, aware that really there is not that much daylight left for them to see the house to make an accurate valuation. Maybe tea isn't such a good idea. They had hurriedly grabbed a Chinese takeout after filming and the contents of Philip's stomach are churning noisily. They are turning in to regular snack jockeys – maybe because neither man had a woman cooking regularly in his life.

"No thank you, Mrs. Menelaws. We are alright. Now if I can get straight to business – Philip and I have looked at the front of the house but we do need to see all rooms and out the back, please, before we sit down and have a chat about what happens next, so can I suggest you show us around?"

"I'll be glad to. Please excuse the boxes down here. Don't know how I accumulated so much stuff. You have seen the front room obviously, so here is the kitchen. It's all fitted out. And yes, please do look at the back garden."

She unlocks the back door and they step grim faced out in to the rain. Sweet little garden, quite well kept with two good trees and flower beds just visible underneath shiny coats of grey-white ice. Good family starter home maybe, thinks Philip. Must fully see the brickwork at the back thinks Scott; boldly scrutinising the entire back of the house for cracks, potential flaws, subsidence, original features, aspects, views. All the usual USPs. All part of the service. But all seems present and quite pleasantly correct. Upstairs though Christine is adamant that a small back room which overlooks the garden *is* a small bedroom, despite the fact that as far as the men knew there hadn't been a bed built yet that could fit in to so small a space.

The lady is pushing it. Probably desperate to sell and make a fresh start, thinks Philip, who thinks he has a pretty shrewd insight in to the female psyche – this despite quite a few females he has dabbled with and left on some other sidelines. Philip measures the room. Scott wanders in to the front bedroom which overlooks the quiet street. Again, a late Victorian built to last number. Nothing remarkable. You could see the woman has cleaned the place recently, yet still there is visible dust on skirting boards. Downstairs the three duly sit down again. It is practically dusk now and Christine snaps on a side light; half drawing the curtains.

"Mrs. Menelaws, what kind of price are you looking at? The market is currently quite slow, but I anticipate no problems selling your property. I'm looking at a sale price of around hundred thousand to a hundred and fifteen. But I'd like to see a copy of the mortgage lease and the first surveyor's report first, please. This is before we place the property details and a photo on our website and deal with enquiries. If you can send us photocopies that should be fine. We charge 20% of the sale price and this charge, as you saw in the literature we sent you, covers brochure costs as well as the actual auction which will be next month. Are there any questions you would like to ask us?"

A brief silence. Scott looks directly at Christine and notices an emptiness about the woman only this time it's an inner emptiness further exaggerated by the pockets of actual bare space in the room. The empty look in her eyes mutates then in to sadness and then in to something else – something he can't quite put his finger on. Maybe a kind of grace. But Mrs. Menelaws has no further questions and agrees to send on the necessaries in the post. "Funny woman, eh?" Philip says as the men drive back in to Edinburgh. "No accounting for taste, but I'd say she was not quite the full shilling." Scott diplomatically remains silent. It isn't for him to speculate on a customer's baggage either literal or metaphorical. Earlier light rain has now become icy torrents and the wind screen wipers are on overdrive. He is due over at Jetta's tomorrow.

Jetta Norton eyes the contents of the can of corn. Fuck. Those nebulous golden sniblets swirling around in milky juice may as well be the contents of her brain right now. Alcohol and love flowed freely with Scott last night in some heady marinated exchanges. But eyeing is not really possible right now: the *twilight* contact lenses she put in last night are playing up, buggering up clear vision. She had wanted to resemble some kind of vampire cat – a kinky treat for Scott.

"Darling, are you awake? I'm free until twelve today but then I must go and see someone in town. *Daarling.* Hope you are not too disappointed. We can meet tomorrow if you like. Sunday I'm not doing anything much at all actually."

A sound of a kettle being switched on, then running water in the bathroom. Jetta places the offending contact lenses in a small glass dish then looks at her real eyes in the mirror. Redness. A small price to pay for the element of surprise. But then, stealthy well designed deceit has always been Jetta's speciality. Whilst other girls at Art School were busy falling off their wedge heels and in to gutters; Jetta's meticulously arranged screws and manipulations only advanced her grades and career. It is all about how one presents oneself, which narrative you used. She is a *nouveau riche* big wig in twee Peebles where her website business is clearly viewed with awe. Her *Naughty Nights with Feathers* items have sold well, particularly in this catchment area. Now China is beginning to bite, she speculates, pouring filter coffee in to two cups and padding in to the bedroom where Scott lies. The early hours of the morning is the best time for dreaming up schemes about global thong domination. And in this brave new world it is she who moves quickest who wins. We are all entrepreneurs now.

"Sweet chicken. Going to lie there all Saturday feeling sorry for yourself?" The question is both question and challenge. For Jetta never has time for wasters or losers. For people who build a monument to their misery and then go worship at it. The Regency flat is done up in chrome, black leather and white walls. So utterly *fantoosh*, darrrling. This is her latest trending word. And the snappy little waistcoat she bought Scott for his birthday yesterday is totally fantoosh. It lies sprawled on a chair in the half gloom next to Scott's lap top. Alone in the flat again, Scott reviews the description of Mrs. Menelaws' property. *Lot 1059.* One bedroomed late Victorian semi, in good condition. GCH, small back garden.

Philip is yet to email him the precise room measurements. A couple of official tax forms sit on the kitchen table. They can wait until later. Official forms always remind him of the coldly formal divorce form he filled out over fifteen years ago. It was strange reading a five line synopsis of his life, his occupation and reason for requesting a divorce. But then forms are never any good at capturing any agony of ambiguity, any shade of grey, any state of transition. Forms seemed so wonderfully sure, so black or white. *How wonderful to be that sure of anything,* Scott thinks, stepping in to a hot shower.

*

The two letters sit on the hall table waiting to be opened. They arrived yesterday morning. Christine thinks she knows what they are, but is in no mood for any more little shocks. Not just now. One is from the auctioneers in Edinburgh; the other has a London law firm's post mark. She had opened another bottle of wine just to cope. *Is this pathetic?* A little voice in her head asks. She had been crying again earlier, before she fell asleep. Watching hopefuls on an afternoon TV talent show depresses her. What, really, are her talents? She's got a talent for memory that is for sure. But somehow memory seems the greatest curse inflicted on the human race right now. She hadn't wanted to remember, she wanted to forget but the wine won't allow it. The last thing she needs today is a day off work, alone with memories. *Lot 1059. A charming one bedroomed late nineteenth century semi, GCH, in good structural condition with fine views and back garden. Near Dalkeith town centre and Country Park, ample amenities nearby. In the region of £100, 000.* Incensed again, Christine reaches for the phone.

"Hello. Is that Mr. Vigour? This is Christine Menelaws. I thought we agreed that the house is two bedroomed – I know the back upstairs room is small but I really think it can double up. Yet you have now placed an advert stating one bedroom. I read it just now. I find this slightly misleading. Can this be corrected please?" She worked hard to keep the slight desperation out of her voice.

"Mrs. Menelaws, I am not happy advertising property under false pretences. Believe me, buyers don't appreciate it. And it is my head and reputation on the block here. The room my colleague and I saw is very small – it is practically a large cupboard – and unless you eat in to some of the landing space which could admittedly be done – that space remains too small really to be called a bedroom. I'm sorry – but there it is. I realise you want the best deal for your property but believe me – so do we. I do hope this answers your query, Mrs. Menelaws. Is there anything else I can help you with today?"

It is unbearable being patronised, even politely. Scott Vigour hung up politely after there had been no other query. Yet she is adamant that they had agreed two bedrooms. Stupid man. She was sure his number plate said '*WUS*' as the two men had driven away in the rain that afternoon. She wondered really what she had to do to be respected. And there had certainly been no respect shown to her by either of *them* when she had seen them again earlier that week. The happy couple. Garry had actually waved to her, yelling from the other side of the street that he'd call her about removing some of his old stuff out from the house. The girl on the other hand just smirked at her with pity. The girl remained a she too as Garry had not even bothered to name her. Maybe it had been him then, trying to get through to her over the last couple of weeks about moving the stuff. There'd been loads of missed calls on the landline. He'd obviously seen the for sale sign out in the front. Maybe he was angry about getting his share of the house sale. It's a fine line though. She ought to call Alan for calm advice. But her landline had just gone dead a couple of times whenever Alan's answer phone was triggered. It made sense given his advanced communication skills.

*

Esmeralda's lips gape at the water's surface back at the Great King Street office. Scott loves feeding her his Aquarian Aquarium food even though he knew deep down that he fed her too much. "You should get the old girl a companion, must be lonely just swimming around by herself," Philip had said. But one fish and one ex-wife cum girlfriend are quite enough females in his life. Esmeralda has served as a scaly transitional good object when he and Jetta were divorcing. Fish are really good at listening to sob stories. Jetta is to meet him later for a Valentine's Day dinner in Glasgow after the auction and there are quite a few properties to shift this afternoon. Good number turning out by the looks of things, over a hundred. He liked this part of the job best – the actual selling. Whenever he is stopped in the street by people asking the inevitable: "Are you that man that presents *What's My Home Worth* on TV?" he always grins and bears it. Perhaps he's become a kind of walking logo. It was difficult enough being an ex-pat in Scotland, one of those smooth Sassenach southerners. Ignorant when first arriving in Edinburgh over twenty five years ago, he had discovered a couple of dodgy train spotter pubs and had virtually apologised personally for Culloden.

He puts on a jazzy polka dot bow tie and rummages for the trusty hammer in the filing cabinet. He and Jetta will spend Easter in London at Jetta's other pad before flying off to Paris for a short break. That phone call last week from that Dalkeith housewife had been bloody irritating though coming as it did after a long fractious enquiry from Saudi Arabia. Mrs. Menelaws sounded distressed and it took all he had not to completely lose it. Anyhow, thinks Scott, driving between the two cities – the property market these days seems to have no national boundaries or loyalties. Everything seemed to be merging into one – and maybe there really was capital in labour and labour in capital as he had heard discussed on the car radio, on one of those topical programmes that analysed the world and its workings since The Second Fall. The other day he sold a virtual coal bunker near Stirling to a foreign customer who paid well over the asking price. Philip will meet him at the venue later.

*

William Bonar and Sons Ltd
Solicitors and Purveyors of Estates
120 Chancery Lane
London EC1 5HP
7th February, 2011

Re: Mrs. Angela Scott's estate and will

Dear Mrs. Menelaws,

We apologise for the delay in writing to you but we have been experiencing considerable difficulty in tracing both details of your deceased mother Mrs. Angela Scott's will as well as the circumstances surrounding your birth. However, please find the attached copy of your birth certificate found as instructed by your assigned solicitor, Mr. James Bonar. After lengthy enquiries, Mr. Bonar was able to obtain a copy of your birth certificate in Broadstairs, Kent where it had been stored at the local Registry Office. Your mother, it seemed, had lost one copy that was rightfully hers during her long residence in London. We therefore formally confirm in this letter that your biological father is a Mr. John Peas and not Mr. Douglas Scott – despite the fact that Mrs. Angela Scott was (and indeed was until the time of her passing) still legally married to said Mr. Douglas Scott.

The marriage between Mr and Mrs. Scott has never been, as far as we have been able to ascertain, formally annulled. Unfortunately, this has implications for your claim to exactly half of Mrs. Scott's estate as her will refers to "offspring and dependents within our marriage" – which would solely describe your brother's claim. You will recall that the will was shown to both you and your brother, a Mr. Alan Scott, when you were last down in London in September 2010. You will also recall that the meeting on September 12th at our offices here was about trying to establish and clarify rightful claims.

If, at a later date, Mr. Alan Scott decides to duly relinquish half of his rightful estate to yourselves then this would have to be drawn up in a separate legal document requiring both of your signatures and a witness. To reduce costs and inconvenience I would therefore suggest one of our partners here as they are already familiar with case detail. I await instructions from your brother and yourself...

The rest of the letter is a blur. Christine knew it may be bad news when she had first seen the envelope a week ago. Doubling up in the hall, she holds her throbbing abdomen.

It's hard to breathe and childhood asthma which she thought she'd well and truly vanquished now returns with vengeance. The phone rings. But this time it is Alan again, sounding insistent yet concerned. She couldn't keep hiding. But now I really am a Miss neither here nor there. I am not even half Scottish. I am married and yet unmarried. *Who the fuck am I then?* she thinks, sitting on the stairs drinking tap water. *Never mind lot 1029, I am the unclaimed, unknown lot.* She planned to meet a colleague in town later, take her mind off the auction. She remembers Chav then, as he laughingly called himself – the homeless poet man she met earlier that week. Three days ago, in anticipation of no Valentine's cards, she bought chocolate hearts in town and had given a couple to a young homeless man sitting nearby. "*Happy Valentines day*" Christine had smiled.

Touched and genuinely surprised, the man grinned cheekily back. "Same to you, my brave daisy lady" he had said, handing her a daisy chain with a grubby hand. Normally she wouldn't chat to beggars as so often they were aggressive. But she liked brave daisy. She asked what his real name was and he said he may as well be called Chav as that's what most people saw. She had laughed. He was so accepting and he seemed sure of himself. All she felt sure of was her own insanity and her own utter insignificance. Walking now to Dalkeith Country Park where Chav is camped out, she remembers a spinning top she had as a child and has hellish visions of herself on it spinning endlessly and repeatedly in history. *Am I really doing the right thing?*

Over cheap cider she pours out her heart and the last six months to Chav and his fellow travellers. They *are* homeless they say. It is true. But they are also protesting against a proposed road. "I don't belong anywhere either," Christine stutters. And Chav gently and drunkenly berates her, assuring her that she does belong and that other daisies will not be able to open as they do should she leave Dalkeith. So it is that she finds herself on a coach to Glasgow hoping to dear God or to something that she will be in time to bid for her own home.

More To It Than Meets The Eye

The hapless lioness looks directly at me for a few intense moments from behind the zoo enclosure fence. It is real eye to eye stuff: man meets animal – King (or Queen) of the beasts meeting with the most dangerous animal of them all: humans. Through the electrifying pinky light coloured rain and steamy vapour emerging from the earth I feel immense shame at being human. I look in to the tawny innocent eyes – the wild large pupil eyes that did not understand anything about conservation, annihilation, genocide – or about war, famine or human greed. The eyes that just saw this two legged creature standing behind a fence. The lion in winter. It had pawed at a log rather sadly, but then, rather amazingly, a powerful primeval roar came from the lion house and all the lions had paced up through the trees and sticks and shrubs to the haunting and commanding sound.

In the growing December dusk at Edinburgh Zoo a distant bell could be heard, warning visitors that zoo gates were to be closed. I turned away, thinking that maybe lions are not the only caged beasts. Looking at the people who were looking at the lions I wondered how free *they* really were – did they allow themselves moments of wildness or were their lives homogenised and safe and filled with efficiently filled out forms and predictable days? The image of the lion stayed with me for a long time; it had touched me in some wordless way. I have a sudden rather horrible thought travelling on the bus back home from the zoo – the thought that humans had actually created their own imprisonment through the phenomena of the enclosed but self conscious and self righteous mind. Unlocking my front door, I almost trip on a pile of letters. It is fully dark now and after a sparse, dry snack of a supper I slowly submit to sleep. My husband rolls on to his back, snoring. Later, in the early hours I find myself tossing and turning; disturbed by my thoughts about modern man. In the darkness outside a wind picks pick up, blowing against the window panes insistently. In the gloom of the room I can just trace the faint outlines of the large white daisies which adorn the wall paper.

I am to catch a coach early tomorrow morning to go to Lincoln and write a piece on the attractions of the city for the newspaper I work for. I work freelance (when I can get the work) and had been asked to do a short write up on Edinburgh Zoo's latest animal instalments – so that was where I had been today. That's when the guilt started. The guilt about being human. I was scribbling away in my note pad and had glanced up, starting slightly at the intensity of the lioness's gaze. Then it began to rain.

My husband had made me some cheese and pickle sandwiches for the journey down. I munch eagerly on one now, staring out the window at open fields and coastline. It is an overcast Friday morning and I was due to return to Edinburgh on the Sunday which, I calculated, should give me enough time to get a sense of Lincoln and its history. I am a bit of a silence junkie and I hoped that my fellow passengers would not be ones who engaged in long or banal conversations on mobile phones. That was one downfall with coaches – you couldn't exactly change seats if the person next to you was determined to infuriate you or bore the arse off you with intrusive questions or vacuous chat. And you didn't have the same freedom of movement on a coach. Still, it *was* cheaper. The Lothian fields scud by and then, just when I think I can enjoy a quiet journey; the piped music starts reminding all on the coach, just in case they had forgotten, that the official 'run up' to Christmas had begun. Every year it is the same; the mass outpouring of sentiment and nostalgia and cards depicting some airbrushed nineteenth century scene – conveniently leaving out some of the more cruel and hypocritical scenes from the past.

For a few brief weeks we can all con or drink ourselves in to thinking that a mince pie and seasonal greetings can make up for squalor, greed and corruption the rest of the year. It is a ritual, a performance. *Thank you very very very much* a man repeatedly sings, accompanied by a small chorus of cheery men and women. I can almost hear a chinking collection tin and a 'Gawd Bless Yer Sir'. The voices sound like actors putting on exaggerated music hall cockney accents. *Rudolph the red nosed reindeer had a very shiny nose.* Even the coach driver is getting in to the spirit of things. Christmas tinsel had been hung in the driver's compartment and a few people were singing along on the coach. Was Christmas just for children? I wasn't so sure. Stopping briefly at some small market town bedecked with lights; it seems to me that in many respects we still are in the nineteenth century. Hell, there were characters from Dickens everywhere and the class system hadn't changed that much. I finish my sandwiches now and try to read a visitor guide to Lincoln.

The Romans founded a military station called Lindum in AD 47 on land that had later become Lincoln. After the legions were withdrawn in about AD 400, a tribe of Angles called the Lindiswaras had controlled Lincoln. The Danes had influenced the city too bringing prosperity through trade. During the middle Ages, trade had flourished further due to the command of the water ways which encouraged trade in wool and wool cloth. Disaster came between April and August 1349 when half the city's population was wiped out by the Black Death. There had been a large Jewish

community in Lincoln, second in number only to London.
Aaron the Jew had been the most famous; lending money
which enabled the building of Lincoln Cathedral and
several other abbeys. Aaron had business interests in nine
shires and his loans to Henry II amounted to more than half
the income of the monarch. That kind of wealth and
influence, though restricted to Jews in money lending only,
was bound to stir resentment, envy, suspicion – and sure
enough, the Jews were expelled completely from Britain in
1290. At the famous cathedral's north transept was an
original round stain glass window known as The Dean's
Eye of around 1220; in the south transept another large
round rosy stained window known as the Bishop's Eye also
helped to keep watchful eyes on church attendees.

I stop reading as I can't take in any more historical
information; the whole city seemed to be crammed full of
history – there would be no shortage of copy to write. I jot a
few notes down. The coach has reached England now; I had
missed the sign saying 'England' though had gathered we
had passed the border due to the excited cheers of my
fellow passengers. The festive music seems to have stopped
for the time being and we are now at some small English
market town.

"Half an hour comfort break only, folks," the driver
announces and I step off the coach with the other passengers
in to the damp December air.

The guesthouse where I am staying in the south of the
city has a bewildering array of smiling, chuckling gnomes
to greet visitors. I have the feeling I am being watched,
maybe not just by the gnomes as I walk up the well kept
path. It is a large Victorian house with a graceful ornate
patio extension. It is late afternoon and I ring loudly on a
door although there are actually two doors – the outer door

being open. A small woman with very dark hair appears in an apron. I say I am the visitor from Edinburgh who called last week to book a room for two nights. She talks a lot and very quickly; asking about the journey down, if I'm on business, what was the weather like coming down and mentioning the fact that she'd been up to Old Reekie once herself. She is a bit too keen to please as she explains business has been slow and I'm breathless just listening to her. She shows me in to a very smart back room, all leather studs and an impressive plant in a brass pot where she explains which room I'll have and the times for breakfast.

The entire guest house looks like a set for Upstairs, Downstairs and yet the décor is not overdone. I sit down, feeling I should listen to her out of politeness but really feeling tired and hungry. What we do in the name of politeness is a source of rich comedy. I answer all the questions, saying no, I had not been to Lincoln before but that I'm writing a small article on the town. "We have leaflets for visitors in the hall and there's a guide book I can lend you," she enthuses, eager to help. I feel exotic – as if I'm a long distance traveller gracing her rooms. Her husband appears then, so I have to repeat the answers. They ask me if I have any special dietary requirements and then tell me that one of the famous twelve Queen Eleanor of Castile crosses had stood near the guesthouse back in the late thirteenth century as King Edward I had had his wife's body taken to a Gilbertine priory to be embalmed nearby.

"Some say the area is haunted. The road nearby is an old Roman road and some say they have seen a cloaked, hooded figure. We don't know who it is people say they saw – a monk, maybe. Eleanor was supposed to be very beautiful and her inside organs were sent for burial in the Angel Choir in the cathedral. You probably know that twelve crosses were erected at the twelve places where the funeral procession stopped overnight."

I wished they had not mentioned inside organs and entrails so soon after mentioning the free range eggs they served but I managed to engineer my way out of the conversation by dropping an artfully placed yawn. She shows me to a very elegant white room with fancy brass bedstead virtually in the roof. I am told the front door is locked at eleven thirty so I can go out and get myself a bite. There are a couple of curry houses nearby, she says.

"The money is up the other end of town, near the Cathedral. That's where we want to be," she offered.

I smiled an acknowledgement, not knowing what else to say at this open statement of aspiration. Good luck to them, I thought. If that is what they want. The bedroom is a decent size with on suite shower and toilet and a lofty view of a nearby scrap of open land and road. At the far end of the patch of open land was a tall line of bare trees. In the summer, you could imagine it forming a wall of leaves and branches but because the trees were bare now you could see the land beyond and a few buildings here and there. Maybe this was the Roman road they meant. Looking at the open land in what was now gathering darkness and mist it was easy to imagine a ghostly monk or ethereal funeral procession. After showering, I check my mobile for text messages from my husband. I've got a pretty good idea as to what I'd like to cover in the piece I am going to write already but seeing some of the town tomorrow will help fill out the gaps a bit. I will take photos and a few notes.

I text my husband, letting him know I am safely arrived and then walk up the very long High Street. People I pass by on the street are muffled up to the chin but I can still catch the excited strains of kids looking at the shop displays. Christmas paraphernalia is everywhere; lights have been attached to street lamps. Great clouds of mist move through the air, visible under the lights. I sit myself down to the sound of sitar music in the *Tandoori Spice* and order a beer. Climbing the stairs discretely in the guest house later, I deduce I am still the only guest. As such, I may have to field more lines of questioning tomorrow morning. The proprietors clearly lived in a separate but adjoining part of the house. It gave the house itself an odd fake feel, as if it was just a theatrical set of a house. I fall asleep slowly half dreaming of mysterious monks and fly by night ancient tragic Queens of England.

My instincts and cautions about the proprietors proved to be correct. They were just a bit too curious about me as a person, what made me tick, my real private opinions – and all this bubbling away underneath an embarrassing veneer. Next morning, over my fresh free range eggs on toast, they quizzed me over my musical tastes, discovering that I originated from London. Did I find the room alright for my needs and was I a fan of musicals, theatre – they asked. The eating area where I sat was unfortunately, open plan which meant one could see them preparing your breakfast in front of you – there was no wall or hatch demarcating boundaries between guests and owners. It is excruciating. There is no escape or emotional privacy, your every nuance and expression is being noted. Did I have family in London; do I go and visit them? I could tell that in *their* minds they perhaps thought that they were making me feel welcome by making polite conversation – but actually they were making me feel more and more uncomfortable. Maybe they were just plain nosey as well as being ambitious and aspirational. I explained that I married a Scotsman and worked free lance as a writer.

No, I didn't particularly like musicals but my parents in law were fans I laughed – desperately trying to lighten the tension. Would I mind if they put some music on softly they asked – but there was a latent hostility and threat in the seemingly open question. I got the impression that if I had said no – they would have started bitching about me as soon as my back was out the door. He put on some Kate Bush, which was pretty loud, then asked if I wanted any more toast or tea.

"Please help yourself to the table," he said, smiling away. His teeth were very straight and even.

"Would I like more spring water?" she asked.

"Your skin looks really beautiful and drinking lots of water is good for your skin, after all."

It is both ingratiating *and* excruciating. They were enough to frighten quite a few away, it was taking customer care too far. Sipping hot coffee, I silently vowed never to return. No, of course I didn't mind music while I ate, I lied. God, I joked, I feel like a right silver spooned lady being waited on hand and foot like this. Really, I'm a grown woman – I can get my own re-fills. She seemed to warm to this comment then, mentioning a certain titled aristocratic lady who they did buffets for.

I sensed a potent ambivalent mixture here of resentment, deference, awe and envy. Some things had not changed since 1290 – when the Jews were driven out. It is the same old shit that goes round, just new targets, new scapegoats. The aristocratic lady in question had the same name as me and I knew they were assessing what *my* exact status was in society. What class was I? As small business people, we really struggle with the way the council wastes tax payers' money they then said, particularly on pretentious arty instalments when really just plain good old fences would do. I remained non-committal. We do have quite a lot of hard working Poles in Lincoln, they added, keen to show they could be tolerant. I smiled and nodded, wishing they could leave me in peace. Finally, they left and I went upstairs to get my camera and note pad.

The fifteenth century Arch of the Stonebow spanning the High Street was the southern gate of the medieval city and definitely worthy of a photo or two. It is brighter today, with patches of blue sky so there is no need for flash. It has been a gateway since Roman times and the chamber above the gateway had been used by the City Council since the thirteenth century. Two robed and elongated figures with curiously placid, dreamy expressions were carved in to niches either side of the archway. Petrified forever in stone, their expressions spoke of some deep spiritual contentment or quiet knowing satisfaction. The unnaturally calm faces showed no sign of anguish, rapture or passion, no process of sacrifice or struggle. The figures, though still aesthetically pleasing and interesting, depicted a lie in a way – in the way that they were complicit in an accepted and acceptable version of history.

Then I pass the Jew's House (though not Aaron's house) on Steep Hill. An outsider's house. A foreign invader. Next door, historians thought the neighbouring house was used as a synagogue. Looking up the hill towards the imposing cathedral you could still decipher how, over time, the hillside had been effectively 'terraced' with layers of buildings spreading out over the centuries beyond old Lincoln town centre. I climb up the hill and eventually come face to face with the enormous west front of the cathedral. The visual detail of the stone is magnificent. It is lace in stone, a kind of layered embroidery of light and shadow. The divine and sublime is set literally side by side with imp, gargoyle and demonic animal. The stones still tell a story, a story of heaven and hell, of good, temptation, redemption and judgement. I pause on the steps, taking it in, writing what I see and consulting the guide book I had brought down with me. A few oriental looking tourists talk excitedly, pointing at the detail in the arches. Incredibly, even in the still chilly December air, a rather tasteful ice cream stall has been set some distance from the ancient hallowed steps. A solitary man huddles in a coat behind the 'stall' which is a kind of fancy big wheel barrow with ice boxes. A kind of close had been created over the centuries, with cathedral on one side and smart eighteenth century town houses with immaculate clipped gardens forming the rest of the enclosure. Had the ice cream stall been any closer to the steps then the sacred would become very obviously and visibly soiled by the commercial – and this could have offended sensibilities. I wondered how he made a living at this time of year.

Just then, as I was wondering if in fact I wanted an ice cream too, a man, woman and child noisily exited the cathedral. The child, a boy of around eight or nine perhaps was strapped tightly in to what can only be described as a harness. The boy is screaming loudly, you cannot make out what he is saying – but clearly he is furious and is having some kind of fit or tantrum. The mother (as I assumed her to be) pulls firmly on the reigns a couple of times and insists that they must go now and that it was no use, the more he screamed the less likely he will get tea later on. There will be repercussions, she warns. The man looks frightened and says nothing. Maybe he never does say anything. Maybe the saying nothing, the compliance and fear is actually saying something – but not in an obvious way. There is a huge temporary silence then in that still cold historic close; the silence hangs in the air almost tangibly – as the ice cream man huddles in his big coat and tries to avoid staring at the child; as the Japanese tourists look anxiously at the ground and divert their eyes away; and as I seeing all this – refuse to simply look away also. Maybe it is the journo in me – I like to try to get to a kind of truth of a situation, the emotional heart of it.

There is a moment when the boy almost seems to realise the embarrassment he has created in the adults nearby, and there is another strange almost an uncanny moment – a don't look now moment or you'll blink and miss it moment – when he senses I am looking directly at him, interested. He turns around, glancing back. Our eyes meet, briefly. I see pain, anger and bewilderment in his eyes – but I also see a high intelligence, a knowing. In short, I see a human animal in another kind of cage – who knows who made the cage and why the restraint was thought necessary. I suspected there were many such fits, screams and yanks on the harness – but I knew nothing of the boy's history, his medical condition or the dynamics in that family. He seems powerless.

Maybe he felt powerless and so had to scream to be heard – thus justifying the harness. What awful thing would happen if the harness was taken off occasionally? The woman yanked him hard then, running out of patience and asserting her control. This set him off again – but then – perhaps that was the whole point. There had been a moment though, just then. Back then. A moment or possibility of something different. There had also been resignation and despair in the boy's eyes as if this was what he always got and this was how he always was. And there was an end to it.

And I go right in to the cathedral and am moved greatly by that small possibility that I thought I had seen. The small falling away of the social masks, of the routine, of the sometimes stifling mundane hypocritical politeness. The amazing arches I walk under now are also lasting testaments to what could be achieved, built, – created – whether by divine hands or human. Or both. *Could anyone hear?* Did the Bishop's Eye see the struggle that people endure, the complexities, the unpalatable truths so awful they dare not scream out their name? There is no photography allowed inside. Looking at the vast stone screens; anything seemed possible and achievable. If only one could allow the idea of possibility of change, be open to the possible. It is hard to completely immerse myself in the glory of the cathedral because the screaming boy's eyes of course are still partly with me in *my* mind's eye – never mind the Bishop's Eye. Were the eyes of the lioness I had seen in Edinburgh really any different from this boy's eyes?

I have seen enough now to get a taste of Lincoln, I feel lucky to have been given this chance, this possibility. I step back outside, out in to the close. The ice cream man is still standing there, stoically. I buy an ice and walk slowly back down the High Street compiling the article in my mind. The editor I work for will give me some leeway but I know roughly the word count I need to deliver. I have more than enough material, I should be able to cobble something together late tomorrow, late Sunday night when I get back. Wonder how the other half is doing, must try and text him, speak to him – share the thoughts on the day. After all, it *is* proving to be quite a little trip, quite a day. More to it than meets the eye in fact.

Mrs. Anderson

In Mrs. Anderson's bedroom there is a built in closet which has doors that double up as full length mirrors. The walls are painted purple and inside the closet and all along one entire wall are hundreds of pairs of shoes, some brand new and never worn. The closet is crammed full of clothes of varying sizes; most of them have never seen the light of day or had an airing. Many of them still have plastic hoops or markers still stapled in to the fabric; some still have stickers on them indicating a sale item. In the desk in the study are whole drawers full of receipts. It was where and how she retained her power. She is a single and small bird like woman in her fifties; she had always loved scouting out a bargain ever since she went to jumble sales as a child.

Her hair is ash blonde; she looks physically delicate – but Mrs. Anderson has a steely will about her and drove a hard bargain at the Princes Street department store she frequented every single day. She knew her consumer rights, she had said to the sales assistant at the refunds desk. These shoes she bought here, at this very store, are faulty. She had not worn them once and they had fallen apart, look. The staff at the refunds desk on the third floor were very well acquainted with Mrs. Anderson; she was a familiar face in that place.

"Good morning, Ron. Caught any shop lifters today, then?" She greets Ron, the security ex-con on the door with a thin little lipstick smile. Ron smiles back, wondering what on earth Mrs. Anderson is on and what motivates her –

Christ, she has been coming to the store – sale or no sale – every day for as long as anyone can remember.

"Searching out another bargain today, then? Chosen a good time, after Christmas and that."

He always looks so rough and unshaved, she thinks, heading straight for the ladies wear section on the fourth floor. Wouldn't want to be pawed by *him*. Rifling through a rack of sale items, she spies a smart pair of grey slacks. Size 12. Bound to fit well with extra room. After all, she knows she is not as slim as she once was. She had taken early retirement from her job as legal secretary and a rich uncle had left her a pot of money when he died. She likes doing The Times cross word and reading Joanna Trollope or Daphne Du Maurier novels. And drinking tea in smart tea shops, chatting to friends who were also of the moneyed leisured class.

"Excuse me, may I have your opinion on this item?" she enquires of a young Asian looking sales assistant who is busy tidying up stock. *Hmm, this is a new girl,* Mrs. Anderson thinks.

"Yes, madam. How can I help you?" the young woman looks warily at her, not wanting a scene.

"Does cotton and polyester mix shrink unduly if hand washed? The only reason I ask this is that I absolutely think these trousers are the right size and shape for me currently, at the point of sale, so to speak. I know it says machine wash on the label, but I prefer to hot hand wash cotton items. I'm concerned about them shrinking either way though."

"I'm sorry, madam. I am not qualified to give you advice on this. Perhaps you would like to speak to the section manager? I would not want to give wrong advice."

The assistant calls to Jean Stockwell, a more familiar face, who then walks over. Hmm. These poor young girls at the store, sometimes foreign – often working the refunds system – *they* were well mannered to her. But those more rounded, mature ladies like Jean Stockwell working on the tills and dressing rooms. Well. They were often jealous. Let's face it – they would never move on from 'shop work.' Mrs. Anderson explains her dilemma to a world weary Jean. Jean has advised her on just about every kind of cleaning, ironing and fabric care enquiry possible. Not for the first time Mrs. Anderson considers how apt Jean's surname is as she eyes the woman's ample bust. You certainly *are* well stocked.

But Jean neither confirms, denies or predicts what will happen to the poor hapless trousers and advises her *that shrinking is a risk we all take when we buy clothes.* In her opinion though, a warm hand wash, as opposed to a hot hand wash would decrease the risk of shrinking. *Well, well. I know that,* Mrs. Anderson thinks, queuing up to buy. Once, during the ubiquitous afternoon trips to the store she had brushed past Mrs. Thatcher in her early glory years in the mid 1980s. "Excuse me", she had said, in that deep throaty voice of hers. Mrs. T had been wearing a thick orangey panstick; maybe she had just had a TV interview. On another occasion, a minor royal had actually been in the queue before her. She realised who it was when she had seen the girl's profile and jodhpurs. The poor sales assistant dealing with the royal was so nervous that a manageress had to come over. Her quick eyes had been right. But then she always spotted the unusual, the really good buys.

Travelling back home on the bus, she recalled the horrifying dream from last night. She was locked in a dressing room with mirrors all around and so could not escape from the image of her own body. There it was in all its lumpish, sagging, puckered reality. More horrifying than this was the shock she had got when seeing how small and shrunken her head was – tiny – compared to the huge elephantine body. Her head was having a hard time just holding itself free and upright from piles of submerging flesh. Total mismatch. The flesh was out of control, spilling out in to the dressing room and threatening an explosion.

For an awful moment she thought she was looking in to one of those warped circus mirrors which were bent in the middle and which blow up your top or bottom half – making you look like an alien or a dwarf with a huge head. But no. The mirror seemed to be pretty normal. There were no kinks. This made the dream even more scary and dislocating. God. She laboured for hours in gyms and drinks green tea to try and maintain herself. And now this. Being forced to confront her failure. Still, she got a great bargain today, and later a nice little Bruntsfield café chit chat with Hilary picks her up.

"What goodies did we get ourselves today, then?" Hilary was such a good friend and listened endlessly to these little battles for decency and customer care. The small café stroke bistro near home was busy with brunch time shoppers and young office types tapping on laptops. The two friends had recently identified a new rather hunky young Italian waiter in the bistro which seems to give the coffee they drink an extra zing.

"A smart pair of grey trousers, cotton and polyester mix mind you – for under ten pounds. I'm going to warm hand wash this evening but there will be hell to pay if they shrink. I'm sure service is not what it used to be, in there. Hold on, he's coming back, Hill, for your order. You naughty thing you. You just want to eye his buttocks again, don't you?"

They laughed together in perfect symmetry, delighted at their sheer ingeniousness, their wiles and wit. The humour however was lost on the waiter, who they discovered is called Giovanni. *What a romantic name they cluck together. And is there a Mrs. Giovanni girlfriend waiting back home in Italy?* The young man flushed and stuttered out an answer while scribbling down the order. They left a generous tip.

Back home, Mrs. Anderson washed her hair, leaving it in an elegant white towel turban. She has the whole house to herself. A Morningside mansion to lose oneself in, and not just in mornings maybe. A house warmed by culture. And whose bloody business was it anyway, what she did with her money, with her time? Let the chattering classes chatter. She knew what they said about her in the store and even, traitors, at the Rotary Club. The trousers were duly hung outside in the small yard area. Spring was in the breezy air, she and Hilary planned a weekend break in Windsor. Weighing herself again on the bathroom scales, she is dismayed to see she has gained a few pounds. She deeply resented Mr. Cochrane's suggestion that she has an eating disorder and ought she to consider seeing a counsellor. It was an intrusion too far; GPs ought to know when to button it. The patient and customers are always right. It is another example of the over care of the nanny state. We taxpayers subsidise these awful intrusions.

*

Mrs. Anderson has this special way of puffing herself up physically when dealing with adversaries. Flight or fight mechanism, often employed by birds. She faces down the young-ish male refunds manager. It's Mr O'Donoghue on duty today and he is well versed in her techniques. "I'm sorry but I was advised that these trousers would not shrink if I washed them in warm water. And yet they *have* shrunk. Now fair enough, if I had washed them in hot water or cold when the label specifically says warm – then yes, I would be asking for trouble."

Mrs. Anderson. Ah, a retail legend. If only they had a surveillance camera up here on the refunds desk, Mr O'Donoghue thinks. That would capture this woman's incredible behaviour. She is the subject of many staff canteen and locker jokes. Some of the comments were cruel, admittedly. He didn't like to speculate on her sex life or social life or lack of it – but still, the woman is a pain in the arse.

"What can I do for you today, Mrs. Anderson? I'm sorry if you were given misleading or confusing advice from one of my colleagues. I'm sure it wasn't deliberate. Can I please take these trousers? I just want to lay them flat out on the counter to see what's what." Mr. O' Donoghue sighs quietly to himself. Really, the staff at refunds ought to get some special award from HQ for dealing with people like Mrs. Anderson. A service award for courtesy beyond endurance. He gives in and refunds the amount in full, despite his qualms about this latest claim. It is more hassle than it is worth, no matter the advice given in management training. Triumphant, she holds her head high as she passes a bemused Ron at the store's ground floor which lead out on to busy pavements.

That night, Mrs. Anderson has another nightmarish dream. Although stuck in the same anonymous mirrored dressing room – this time it is her head that is absolutely huge in proportion to a tiny shrunken body. My god! Her body looks skeletal. It is quite extraordinary. Where has the flesh gone? Huge staring eyes gaze at her from the alien distorted head. She tries to open her mouth to scream but nothing comes out. She bangs on the walls but nobody comes. A metal grille in the floor in a corner catches her eye and she steps precariously over on tiny shrunken feet – feet that look like the feet of a child. Looking down through the grille she sees endless pairs of feet in shoes walking by on a pavement. Young feet, old feet. Court shoes and lace ups. She stamps loudly on the grille, but nobody can hear. Sweating, she wakes in the early hours. Panic ridden, she switches on the bedroom light and once more examines her body in detail in the full length mirror. Phew. All seems to be present and correct. Nothing out of place or out of proportion. *You silly moo. It is just a bad dream.* A crossword helps her to sleep.

At the café with Hilary Mrs. Anderson laughs at herself again. Getting herself in to a tizzy over nothing. They spy Giovanni before he sees them and decide to order cake to celebrate this latest small conquest. Digging in to thick indulgent cake, she remembers with satisfaction the look on Jean Stockwell's face as she had successfully gone over her authority to seek the refund manager. That was well played. You could see the humiliation on her face. Silly bitch.

It is endlessly entertaining, these small battles. Turning in to her street later though, she knew instantly that something was wrong. Two police cars are parked outside the splendour of her Georgian town house. Frightened, she scurries up the steps to the front door. A police officer at the door asks if she lives here.

"Yes," she replies. "Anything wrong?"

"'Fraid so," says the copper. "Your home has been ransacked. Jewellery, electrics and lots of clothes nicked. Sorry, madam. Unlucky."

Pamela and the Beetroot

Not very far from Corstorphine Hill in West Edinburgh there are a series of roads with small neat terraced houses built in the late nineteenth century. The slates on these roofs are the original grey-black ones and each roof is a mini masterpiece in harmonious alignment, each roof a testament to the skilled hands of yester year. A row of mature plain trees in these modest streets mirrors and compliments the neat rows of box like houses and in some of the back gardens other trees branches have become rather overgrown and even tap regularly on some residents' windows when the winds are high. Life continues in an orderly manner within these streets: cars leave and arrive with clockwork mechanical precision despatching children to schools and taking people to offices and workplaces. No dog shit, litter or bikes plague these pavements, and whilst not being exactly affluent or posh – one could safely say these streets and homes were at least respectable. And so this was the state of play *without*.

A small Asian run corner shop at the end of one of these cosy little roads comes in handy for milk, bread and papers – and it is in this shop that Pamela Macleod, seamstress, shop assistant, wife and mother combined fumbles for change in her purse. Finding the loose coinage at last, she pays the proprietor and walks the five minute walk home in what appears to be a bright blustery March morning. She is to work flexi time later that day at the Haymarket shop with Sybil, the owner. It's only a bus away.

Radio weather forecasts earlier that morning promised mixed blessings but Gordon Macleod shrugged it off in his hardy stoical manner, driving off to work as usual. No amount of extreme weather prohibited his appetite for work. They had been married for over ten years now, and for ten years Pamela had dutifully made packed lunches, fed and comforted their petulant teenage daughter Daisy, and generally tried her utmost to be a good wife and mother. Gordon travels a lot as he owns a household removals company, a solid Edinburgh family business now in its hundredth year. Reputation had grown successfully over this time and, as a consequence, work often took him and his team to just south of the border as well to large parts of the north of it. Today's trip involved an overnight visit to Perth and Pamela prepared for yet another solitary evening in with spicy Mexican corn chips, DVDs and herself.

Daisy, strident ladette in ultra short mini skirt somehow has and yet has not flown the parental nest and in between the frequent comings and goings is often to be found semi-camping out on boyfriend's Max accommodating bedroom floor. Technology in all its weird and wonderful manifestations has penetrated the Macleod household and time is now meta regulated super efficiently for twenty four hours, day and night. The all consuming Internet's presence graces virtually every room and there are mobiles, gaming devices, life style organisers and now, much to Pamela's incredulity, pieces of handheld software enabling husband and crew to view street destinations, all courtesy of satellite dishes.

Morning evolves in to afternoon as mornings do and the only dishes Pamela contends with are a large pile in the kitchen sink which has been lovingly left by daughter and husband. She is to start work at Miss Sew and Sew at two: enough time to check for mobile texts and take the old bacon and cheese quiche for a short walk. Gathering up the small hound's leather lead hanging in the hall way, she could not honestly remember when exactly the Macleod family had started to call the yellowy-white West Highland terrier the bacon and cheese quiche; she had a vague idea that it may have been when they first got him. Locking the front door with mobile and dog lead in her other free hand, she realises with a shock that she is actually glad to leave the house. For years the home, the house, the castle – had been a safe haven, a sanctuary and in the early child free years of the marriage, before the endless grind of housework, she had taken pride in their home. She was not entirely sure if any of the housework would ever get done should she die suddenly. In her mind's eye she suddenly has a vision of herself ironing angrily at ninety and the idea horrifies her. And so this was the state of play *within*.

Bertie, the bacon and cheese quiche makes a sudden lunge for freedom and space as they approach Corstorphine Hill and Pamela releases the desperate dog and switches on her mobile. *Be back tomorrow around eight. Don't forget to call office about cleaner's pay.* An on going dispute over the cleaner's pay is driving Gordon up the wall and lucky old Pamela is to call the company secretary to try and negotiate a pay settlement peacefully. Gordon said it needed a woman's touch to sort it. He is a very proud, silent man – she had thought him considerate when they had first married but had realised slowly that he was either not willing or not even able to articulate emotions the way she craved. A huge tense chasm had somehow grown up between them, unawares.

Bertie is panting and pissing right up against an old oak tree trunk which has clumps of daffodils blooming around it. Steamy dampness lingers in the air threatening rain but she is still glad of these small snatched pockets of sanity, away from pressures, expectations, routines. The trees are very dense on this part of the ancient hill, they almost block out skylight. Witches had been burnt very near this spot, according to local folklore. Robert Louis Stevenson had set a scene in Kidnapped near here too. She starts slightly as she steps on a brittle twig, snapping it clean through. Do the trees have eyes and ears, she wonders? Maybe they had witnessed the screams of the cursed, the trapped and the hunted.

*

The bus comes quickly and Pamela hops on, thankful to avoid the rain which has started to come down now in fresh silvery torrents. She had never minded walking in the rain as a child, never had the prudish fear of getting wet – aware even then that people can hurt you far more than mere water can. She was a sensitive, unusual little girl, much to her deceased mother's annoyance. A teenager sitting downstairs on the bus near to her is playing a CD rather too loudly and the bus driver tilts his head and has words with him which seems to do the job.

She and Sybil have a big wedding order to deal with which will involve semi manic machining and a fair amount of embroidery by hand. They need to make serious head way with this today and tomorrow, she thinks with a sigh, visualising the large mound of lace and sequins she had left last week. Still, Sybil can be a laugh to work for, all five foot three of her, as well as being a shrewd, albeit eccentric business woman. Pamela remembered when she had first stumbled across the shop; over ten years ago it had been now. She was walking down near Shandwick Place with a six year old Daisy in tow and they stopped to admire some pretty wee pin cushions and sparkly buttons. They had got on well, Pamela and Daisy then, until the dreaded pubescence and teenage angst. Daisy had a fondness for bananas, as a bairn and Pam indulged her often leading to the inevitable nick name 'banany-mammy'. Sybil had been dressed in an electric blue dress with matching blue mascara and earrings, *Aquarian blue* she had said to Pamela. They had got talking about astrology, bringing up children and trying to earn money. One thing led to another and Pamela mentioned she was looking for work. Sybil had been glad of an assistant.

"You look very thin, hen. Sure you are remembering to eat enough yourself, what with all that cooking you do for family?"

Sybil has an odd little habit of clicking her tongue against the roof of her mouth. She is sitting by a really huge antiquated looking sewing machine: all Edwardiana in black and gold, which contrasts with the brilliant dark pink of the taffeta she is working on. Sybil always pins her black hair up in a fifties style chiffon and claims to be able to read a woman's bra size from across a room. This uncanny ability had come from years of working in the best fitting rooms in London and Paris.

Pamela is never sure if Sybil is asking questions or just making observations about her. She knows Sybil had quite a past with men. Her shop is a treasure trove of boxes, ribbons, material on big cardboard rolls. A large elegant shop window artfully displays further wares. The job is going pretty well, but they had to finish the finishing touches on the dresses and bouquets by the end of the week.

"Tell Gordon he should do the cooking. Do him good. Or better still get the daughter to do it. Can you pass me the small embroidery scissors? You ought to go away for a dirty weekend or a girls' night out. Go and have some fun. And make us another coffee, will you? One sweetener, ta."

Pamela works through her own pile of alterations. When the soon to be bride arrived in the shop with rough designs a month ago, she had been privately revolted by all the froth, pomp and lace. There really is no accounting for taste. *Are you really sure of what you are getting in to?* she had felt like saying at the time. *You look too naïve and young to be married.* She buttoned her lips though through force of habit, a habit she had learned when young. People did not want to hear some things it seemed. At the back of the shop there is a small round mirror and Pamels peers at herself, noting with a start the long blonde hair peppered now with grey. It seems to her suddenly that her eyes are silently screaming something, something she cannot hear.

At home she makes the all important call to the office cleaner, getting what sounds like the giggling cleaner's daughter on the line. She leaves a message and half an hour later neighbour Morag calls to remind her of the Church Easter Cake Bake sale, now looming threateningly on the horizon. It didn't look as if Daisy had been home but at least Bertie is pleased to see her. *Have you called Audrey yet? Had a good day,* states Gordon's text on her mobile. Dicing vegetables, Pamela forgets the day.

The playboy bunny ears have been left provocatively on Pamela's dressing table. She had not heard Gordon come in: but then that is his way. Silent but potent. It seemed to Pam that a lot of men were like this. Still waters running deep. Hidden passions. She finds him down stairs working on the company accounts whilst listening to a CD.

"What's cooking, good looking?" he asks, flicking off the CD and eyeing her in her tight jeans. They had not had sex for nearly two weeks. He pulls her towards him and on to his lap.

"Guess who bought mummy bunny some bunny ears for April Fool's day? Mister bunny is feeling as horny as a rarebit."

He is nibbling at her ears, laughing. There were these brief moments of intimacy when things were easy and luminous, when they both unfolded like flowers to one another. At other times a huge silent abyss opened between them again and Pam felt as if she was a virtual whore running a hostel of some kind. They lie in bed upstairs in the growing darkness and he traces her profile with his large practical hands. He had insisted that she wear the bunny ears as a laugh and she knew that he was invited occasionally to strip clubs along with his work mates. His lovemaking is primordial and intense.

After, he lies gazing enigmatically at the ceiling while Pamela wonders if she ever really knew this predatory side to Gordon. *Do we ever really know anybody?* the hysterical American rape victim had said in the slasher-horror flick she had watched on TV late the other day. The line had struck something deep in her. Later that evening, Daisy solemnly appears with dirty laundry declaring that she is pregnant with twins. Seeing Pam's shocked face, she sticks out her tongue. *Gotcha, April Fool.* Before she can say anything Daisy has disappeared again down the hall as silent and stealthy as a young lynx. She never seems to be able to get a word in with either of them. With dawning horror she realises that the Church Cake Bake and indeed the whole production that is Easter itself is only two weeks away.

*

The church hall is littered with cakes on fancy paper doilies, painted eggs and daffodils. Morag is doing a last minute check over the goods and is preparing to man the tills. She always looks incredibly tanned and fit all year round probably because of the sheer number of times she is always flying abroad with her property developer husband. Clusters of chatting women and excited children mill amongst the wares on the tables. With a sinking heart Pamela tips out her culinary creation from a tin. The cake, as usual for her, has sunk rather badly in the middle and is really too moist for a sponge. It happens every single time no matter how carefully she follows the recipe. For a brief moment she had thought about buying a cake from a bakery and just faking it. Is it really worth the hassle?

Although never openly admitting to very unchristian thoughts, the women secretly got very competitive about the cake making. Somehow, it was another hallmark, another marker or indicator of feminine success or failure. Then again, St. John's has always felt oppressive to Pamela – perhaps now more than ever. It is a typical gloomy late Victorian number, very Presbyterian and the Minister is always preaching about the work ethic and helping those less fortunate. Somehow though, the ministry always felt hypocritical and patronising. Morag wanders over too casually to inspect Pamela's contribution. It is always humiliating dealing with Morag, who is reigning Corstophine Cake Queen. To top it all, Pamela can feel her nether regions leaking rather badly. After exchanging a few pleasantries, Morag goes subtly for the kill. It is all in the tone, in the suggestion.

"I am sure I saw Gordon the other day with what looks like your office cleaner whizzing around in that van of his. Is he still away quite a lot because of work? I think you said you had a few issues with staff pay, didn't you? Must be difficult. They *can* be difficult to sort. Charles and I had a similar problem with a builder we hired a few years ago."

Take a hike, Pamela thinks. You are a walking fake bake woman if ever there was one. You probably wrap your knickers in kitchen foil too.

"It could well have been Morag. Gordon quite often gives Audrey a lift because she has trouble with her veins." Pamela tried to keep her tone matter of fact and disinterested as Morag continues her inspection.

"This was definitely a much younger woman that I saw though. Maybe you are hiring temps too?" Morag saunters off gleefully, hopeful that a little poisonous dart has been implanted in Pamela. Disgusted, Pamela flees to the ladies' room. *Whatever happened to my life,* she silently mouths to herself. Emerging back in to the hall, she turns around abruptly and picks up her coat; walking out past the altar, aware of the looming wooden presence of the lord and his sacrifices on the cross. *Fuck it,* she thinks. *I cannot endure this pretence any more.* Outside in the fresh air she hums a little song to herself. Christ, it has been years since she sang she realises. *I have forgotten the sound of my own voice.* It is on the bus home that she realises she has left a bloody tampon wrapped in toilet paper in one of the church's discreet cubicles. Well it is all too late now. It is surely the final sign of her deviancy and failure.

Morag's poisonous dart penetrated deeply over the next few weeks; spoiling the whole of April. That is surely the point of verbal darts after all – Pamela knew well the power of words. How could anyone imagine that words couldn't hurt and that sticks and stones alone could break a person, she thinks? Alone again in the kitchen, Pamela remembers the cruel playground taunts; the taunts about these stones and sticks and being the King of the Castle. It was always about status, always about the toxic, spiteful dumping that humans inflict on others. Stabbing at baking potatoes, she realises she is furious with Morag. It was if a powerful explosive light bulb had been switched on suddenly inside. Morag had been trying for years to undermine her. The seemingly perfect neighbour appeared to be consumed by a kind of jealousy and there was no escape from this corrosive worm, even here in nice leafy suburbia where everyone makes great show of being polite.

Where is the safety and comfort in this world? She cries to the silent kitchen walls, to the baking potatoes, to a bemused Bertie who is quietly observing her movements from his hairy dog basket in the corner. Tears flow as she berates herself bitterly for her terrible crippling blindness. And then there is Gordon. The mobile text arrived late last night after they had rowed and he had driven furiously off in to the heady cherry blossom filled night. *I think it best if we get a divorce* said the single devastating line. He had hit her and a lovely purple bruise is developing organically around her eye. She hadn't recognised him last night; it was if she was looking at a total stranger.

The hardy, stoical man she had been living with in this house for over ten years had mysteriously gone and there was a strange new savage fire in his eyes. This man who had fathered their child, whose rough large hands once excited her with their tenderness. She had seen him and Audrey's daughter leaving the office late last week. Morag's dart had eaten away at her insides, mutating in to a parasitic worm rotting her guts and terrorising her. She had seen them driving off together in his van, the young woman all dove eyed awe. *Oh why couldn't I see it before? Can anybody really hear me now in my utter desolation?* Seeing the wine in the fridge, she is unable to stop herself.

The baked potatoes are burnt through and with it all pretence of normality. Time is a dismal suspension, her head an overheated telephone exchange. Lying pissed on the kitchen floor, she is dimly aware of the fact that she has pissed herself in the pants too. She is a nyaff, a worthless midge on the face of this barren earth. The architecture of the day had begun smoothly right enough, with precision actually, but now she had finally fallen completely in to the ever waiting hungry abyss. With hindsight, she always had been aware of the abyss lurking menacingly at the back of some room in her mind.

So there *is* an abyss within too, as well as the abyss without with the man she called husband. A minor miracle she hadn't been admitted in to some mental institution years ago, frankly. Earlier, walking round to the corner grocery store again, she had seen some luscious looking beetroots and had felt oddly compelled to buy some from kind old Mr. Singh, who nodded his turban head at her. The intense purple closely matched her bruise, now gradually subsiding underneath thick pan stick. If she bumped in to Morag again she feared she would assault her violently. There was just something about that shade of deep purple in the beetroot. Something about the colour, the smell and the distant memory of seeing plants growing.

Last night, before blacking out, she dreamt of her elderly father's leafy vegetable allotment in Preston Pans. He had won prizes for his beetroots. She *had* known brief moments of happiness as an unselfconscious girl; unaware then of her expected future role as a woman. It was a process this forgetting to then remember. She had forgotten the smell and feel of earthly things, there had been space to dream then. Slamming the door violently, Daisy and Max are led up the hall by Bertie, looking as cute as a big girls' blouse. Unlike Daisy, *he* had been such a comfort to her in her long over night hours of silent writhing agony.

"Are the potatoes ready, mum? Bertie ran off up the hill after some bitch on heat so we chased him."

Daisy discreetly turns a blind eye to the beer cans on the kitchen floor, but sharp eyed Max spots the ash tray full of cigarette stubs which Pamela had somehow not got round to emptying out yet. A faint whiff of lager and fags still hung in the kitchen air. A tall striking looking teenager, Max's aquiline nose always detects odd smells and the unusual. Daisy has recently acquired the habit of wearing sparkly eye make up which distracts attention away from what her eyes are saying. Pamela knew that Daisy had sensed deep marital trouble a while ago, but like her father she simply hardened up and withdrew.

It is a slap in the face, a terrible jolt to see exactly how contemptuous both her husband and daughter are of emotion, let alone the expression of emotion. Daisy's eyes are hard dangerous glinting flints in the kitchen light. And she had once held this person in her arms and comforted her in the dark; this challenging young woman who now stands before her. The relentless abyss has claimed a new victim: this would be woman, this woman yet to be – is now also, it seems to Pamela, thrown in to some unknown moral orbit. Bluebells bloom in the garden, visible through the kitchen window.

Now May had just appeared, Pamela did not know where from. She knew she must try and say something to diffuse the terrible tension in the room. That she did know. Daisy is waiting for an answer, Max looks curiously at her. One must account for oneself and give reasons. Technology is always good for that of course, she realises with relief. *I must be here and this must be really happening because that man, Gordon – well, he sent me a text I think it was yesterday telling me it is all over. And now there is this terrible silence in this room and I am expected to answer, to give an account of what happened to the baked potatoes.*

"The potatoes are burnt, actually," Pamela said flatly, staring off in to space. All this endless relating and explaining is draining the living sap out of her. She feels dizzy in the ominous silence. Gordon had texted again since that awful night to say he needed to pick up some clothes and his laptop. She did not want to be in the house when he let himself in to the house with his own spare key. It is all too awful. She had puffed furiously on a scrounged fag butt earlier that morning as she watched some lurid early morning chat show. The topic for discussion had been parasitic single mums on welfare who sat around at home all day feeling sorry for themselves. She had switched the TV off instantly; determined to finish the fag.

"What will we eat then, Max and I? I thought you said you'd put potatoes on. There isn't even any bread to make toast." Daisy slams the bread bin shut, staring angrily at her mother. Bertie's ears prick up, anticipating danger.

"I guess you will just have to go and eat elsewhere. What can I do?" The words somehow just fall out of Pamela's mouth before she even knew it. Lord. What woman was this that now spoke this way – maybe she too is one of the cursed barren outcasts to be purged and burnt on Corstorphine Hill. It is just a matter of time before society would make its judgement.

"What kind of fucking joke mother are you anyway? Look at the state of you and this house. You know what?

I'm actually embarrassed to live here. Come on, Max – let's get the hell out."

Daisy stomps furiously off with Max trailing behind her. Before Pamela can cry out Bertie runs through the front door which is left open in teenage defiance. A murderous screech of tyres, a whelp of pain and Bertie is fighting suddenly for his life in the middle of the road.

*

Sybil is on the phone, putting on her best posh English department store voice. She is ordering more taffeta for yet another wedding. It seems the previous happy young bride to be has recommended Sybil and her unassuming assistant. Sybil is buzzing excitedly; word of mouth custom is always a feel good factor. And it is always good to hear Sybil laugh and click her tongue again; it is genuine. Say what you will about Sybil's dress sense or colourful past with men: you always knew what you were getting. Like it or lump it. She has heard it all now from Pamela; she had dug and dug until it all came out in a tearful torrent. Half jokingly, Sybil offers to make her some voodoo dolls to stick pins in.

"It will get better, I promise you," Sybil had said and she looked in one of her weekly astrology guides to see what the stars foretold for Pamela.

Today honesty will release you and you will be unburdened, the guidance said. Miraculously, Pamela finds herself laughing. Sybil kindly suggested she take some paid time off work. The divorce papers arrived yesterday but she had not been able to deal with them or deal with anything really. Not since poor Bertie. After she had buried Bertie's shattered remains in the back garden she had felt the need to once again take the walk alone up Corstorphine Hill. Leaves had appeared, the air is warm anticipating summer.

The world is coming alive again, oblivious to her dead heart. She could not even begin to think about what would happen to the house yet. It became a house of perpetual worry towards the end she cries, thinking about how hard little Bertie had fought for his life. It is so unjust. She passes a young man in trainers up at the hill top who sees her distress. *Tough luck love, that's life,* he mutters, sauntering off in immaculate white chav trainers. His spit wobbles on the ground. *We live like brutalised pigs,* Pamela thinks. *Pigs in a quietly savage asylum of an Island.* Looking down at the view below, she saw the neat rows of little houses with the neat regulated little lives. She spent so much of her life there.

Seen from afar it seems a kind of farce this human condition, but actually living in it close up is a tragedy. Max will visit later and they will share a few stolen hours of passionate screwing. It happened when she had broken down; sobbing in the road over Bertie's dying body. Daisy stood incapacitated by horror, silenced for once. A sympathetic look of understanding between Max and herself and now she is an adulterous single mum nervously watching the gap in the front room curtains – timing her visits to the corner grocery store meticulously to avoid Morag's moral glares and intrusive questioning.

It occurs to Pamela that Morag may well have seen Max arriving and departing at all hours; Daisy doesn't know about them yet but by all accounts she has given up on her mother and has taken her now absent father's side. She is staying with a friend and has regular contact with her father Gordon by mobile. Walking down the hill, Pamela concludes that technology is another kind of entrapment, another way that people could monitor, track and regulate you. Before Max arrives she drowns the mobile phone in a ritual bath.

*

Maybe the beetroots will save her. She often thought of her father's wee greenhouse and vegetables at the Preston Pans allotment. He gave her a flower fairies of the garden book when she was small and she was hooked. She sees her reflection in the bus window and the way the dyed aubergine streak in her hair catches the light. The dye left tell-tale stains on the pristine white pillows – but no matter, Gordon's very quiet tyranny had ended. It had been such a regulated, stifling existence. The house is nearly sold, its furnishings going to pot. God, she smiles to herself thinking again of poor old Bertie. *Maybe I too am just a sad old dog on heat.* It was the ladybird in the front room that inspired her, an unusual orangey one with white spots. That and some uncarthly music she thought she heard reverberating through the May air; calling her back to the vegetables and the greenhouse. Her feet will take her there, she could at least be sure of this. Hell, she might even one day become accustomed to this living inside out.

Shit Happens

Usha Stockbridge, fifty three, had worked in the ladies' public toilet in St. Andrew's Square for nearly seventeen years now. She had married a white Scotsman, a fact that her Asian parents did not like initially but had gradually come to terms with. Relations between her parents and her husband had grown organically into a kind of silent mutual tolerance as early explosive rows and disagreements were exhausting for all parties – let alone for Usha who felt like a cross between a referee and pig in the middle. It had been a bloody, long and hard struggle for Usha who had to endure emotional abuse from a screaming mother and complete rejection from her father and her father's extended family. She was a black sheep of the family; a scapegoat used to taking shit. *Bad daughter* or so the judgement went. So it was fitting, in a way, when she had got the job with the council as a lavatory attendant which involved, amongst other tasks, the daily clearing up of shit, urine and sanitary towels left floating lazily in working toilet bowls.

She had heard and read about the intimidation and bullying heaped upon other Asian women; particularly Asian women who had daringly chosen a husband of their own. Usha knew why many Asian women were silent, afraid. It was not just about culture. Growing up in Bangalore, she had heard about the United Kingdom but she had heard only good, magical and polite things. She lives quite near her work, about twenty minutes away, in a big drab grey block of flats. She walks to the square and the public toilets every morning and every evening except on three precious gold dust weeks in the year when the only toilet she walks to is her very own pink Armitage Shanks in the privacy of her very own home. On these free dream time days she remembers again the sacred monkeys and lush forests of home.

Usha puts on heavy eye make up; it is part of her daily morning ritual. It is part of who she is, even after all these years living here. It can never be taken away from her. Thick black kohl lines appear around her eyes in the brightly lit bedroom mirror. Lenny, her welder husband has copped off to work already. He had been working briefly on the dreaded trams but the contract ran out. He also works for the council but it is shift work so he will not be back until late. She will leave him a warm macaroni pie with chips in the oven. She has practically given up wearing a sari now except for special occasions. She remembers that she must call her daughter this evening when she gets back from work and that there is no fruit or bread left. Her one daughter has gone back down south to Leicester with Usha's parents to study at university.

She has laundered her blue overalls and there is a good supply of pine disinfectant in the small cupboard under the little sink which is in the lavatory attendant's room. Her supervisor, a big friendly bosomy woman called Cheryl does not mind if she listens to Asian radio stations in the afternoons if all is quiet. Cheryl, the Council Supervisor visits Usha every three weeks just to see how she is getting on and to note supplies. She is required to enter any incidents in the black incidents book so the council can keep an eye on staff health and safety and welfare. When the toilets are quiet and all the cleaning is done, Usha sings and embroiders along to the best of Bollywood pounding out from a stereo cassette player she has installed in the attendant's room. She is transported mystically then, transported by the music across land and sea to India's surging heat and colours; transported to the supreme. In her way she is an untouchable then. Sometimes she feels as if she is only half on British soil anyhow; as if her heart was buried deep by an ancient mountain.

Walking the familiar route to work she wonders what unsavoury little deposits she will be clearing later today – she had left everything immaculate late last night but by late afternoon today who knows what debris will have built up. Condoms. Pill packets. Beer cans. Nappies. Sodden fag ends soaking in toilet water. Coppers and small change which she had saved over the years in a large urn at home. And of course, crap in all shapes and forms. It is a bright clear day in May and Usha appreciates the beauty of the delicate cherry blossom trees that blow their pink petals everywhere, like blessings. Her blouse ripples in the breeze. Most of the time she had been able to live her escaped life in blissful post- parental peace but there had been a couple of times when the word 'paki' had been hurled abusively at her from passing cars or in supermarkets. There was no point in telling these people she wasn't even from Pakistan.

It was just idiot wankers, her husband said. She should not worry or be frightened, but hold her head high and keep on walking with dignity. When they had first arrived here, years ago, she had cried at night, terrified. Her husband had rocked her to sleep in his arms, like a bewildered baby. She prayed to Hanuman and Krishna then who comforted her and told her while she was asleep, that, as in the holy scripts, everywhere there is karma and soul re-cycling on the big dramatic wheel of life. So there is no need to fear the shit or dirt – whether it is calculated abusive shit or random shit. Shit is shit, it is matter that occurs. It will happen, whatever you do. It is part of life and it will not go away. But you can react with dignity. It is just people living their karma that is all. The wheel will turn again, sure enough.

Accept that the shit will happen. It is in the very nature of things.

Usha gets to the toilets at 8am sharp and unlocks the front entrance door with the heavy duty council keys. Putting her bag on the little table in the attendant's room, she does a little mini check on all the toilets. All is well. Once, in all her years of service she saw a big rat hurrying out of the front door first thing in the morning when she had arrived: it must have been hiding somewhere. She had screamed and dropped her bag. But then she laughed at herself. It is just a creature, doing what creatures are bound to do. It had to survive somehow. You could not really blame it. When she wedged the toilet entrance door open in the long hot summer months, pigeons that had been wandering for scraps elsewhere in the square had sometimes wandered then in to the toilets so she had chased them away with a mop. And sometimes the bin men popped their head round the door to say hello which of course was always nice and friendly and welcome. She checks under the sink for detergent and clean cloths and gloves. Sitting down with a cup of hot sweet tea and biscuits, she puts on her reading glasses and embroiders a skirt all morning. "I am a street danceeeer, I am a street danceeer" the cool pop mantra has her jolting her head along in time. Later on she is expecting a delivery of toilet rolls and liquid soap.

*

In the late afternoon, through the discreet two way mirror in the door of the attendant's room she notices a young blonde woman coming in to the toilets. There had only been two women visiting the toilet all morning, but it was only early in the week and things tended to become more hectic as the week wore on. Friday and Saturday nights were the dodgy times. Then she notices a really dishevelled pasty looking woman coming in who sways about on her legs. A druggie. For some reason they loved to congregate and score here. The police and council had been understandably reluctant to install CCTV cameras as there would have been a public outcry about privacy. The blonde woman screams "lesbo perv" as the druggie woman flashes a little mirror in blue painted nails under the cubicle dividing walls to get a closer look at the blonde woman wiping her privates. Unbelievable but true. You couldn't make it up. You are potentially fair game even when spending a penny. Usha opens the attendant's room door then and firmly yanks the druggie girl away from the cubicle door.

The druggie girl puts up a fight but Usha has developed a technique and straddles the girl's back between her powerful thighs, pinning her face down to the floor. The language is appalling but Usha is used to it now. This type of verbal shit and abuse had a pattern to it, a kind of relentless logic. She'd been spat at often enough too. The young blonde woman meanwhile has emerged from the cubicle next door looking shaken. She offers to call the police from her mobile but Usha says she can call, it is okay. But she must stay in the toilets, please, as she is a witness to this. She must stay to make a statement. Usha calls from the mobile which is clipped to her blue overall – all the while restraining the writhing druggie with all her might. The smart young blonde woman looks on, stunned yet admiring. She has never seen anything like this before. It is better than reality TV. The police arrive and the girl gives a witness statement and they drag the screaming, protesting druggie off with the blonde girl gawping behind them. The rest of the day passes off uneventfully and around seven thirty Usha finally gets home and flops down asleep.

She wakes later in the evening and speaks to her daughter in Leicester briefly. She is doing well at university, hoping to become an accountant like her maternal grandfather had been before he retired. Usha's father did not think much of welding as a profession. He had to work hard, damn hard in India and in England to qualify as an accountant. It was a source of eternal shame to him that Usha had married a mere welder – a white welder to boot – and was only a humble lavatory attendant living in Scotland. But Usha was always rebellious, determined to make her own mistakes and to be free from her oppressive father. She had fought her own private battle: a fight for the right for her own identity, her own happiness – no matter how mundane.

*

The public toilet where Usha works looks like a large concrete TARDIS from Doctor Who, or maybe an outsized re-cycled 1960s police box that used to be functional across the city. She kept the place spotless for as long as she was able to, which sometimes was not for more than a couple of hours. Her own small little attendant's room with a stripy two way mirror in the door masquerading as glass also had a chair, a wee kettle and a vase full of garish plastic flowers. A statue of Hanuman the monkey God stood on guard on the small window ledge. She had seen much through this glass over the years. She wondered if ordinary people she passed by everyday would believe some of this behaviour. Occasionally there were young student types fucking and shooting up in the toilets; they looked smart and self assured *outside* walking around on the streets right enough – but inside the toilets was another matter. The masks fell away here and relieving oneself is always a great leveller like death. Some students became prowling hoydens at night, screaming like banshee cats.

It was a strange kind of egalitarian free for all in the toilets – anything went and all social pretence; all the cosmetic niceties and the masks of status, social class and assumed identity might have been just flushed away. On one occasion she had nearly been beaten up by a couple of big punky looking lesbian women in black boots who had been daubing the wall with obscenities. And on one awful full moon August night about five years ago, three drunk men had swaggered in to piss and flash their dicks at the women.

Now that had been terrifying and she had silently asked Hanuman and Krishna for help. The men cornered one young woman in a cubicle and would not let her out. Usha had to call the police then on the direct number she kept securely cello taped to the telephone in the attendant's room. She tried to humour them and asked them politely to please use the men's toilets which were nearby, but they were not having any of it and one of them promptly spat on her. The police had arrived pretty quickly but it had been a real private terror for her going to and from work for a while afterwards as one of the blokes had threatened to come back and "batter her". They knew where she worked of course. Since that episode she always kept a mobile phone on her on both her husband's and the police's insistence.

The council, to their credit, had provided both health and safety training and had hired in a self defence instructor for their employees – it seemed that many staff in front line jobs dealing with the public now suffered increased risk of violence and assault to their person. Usha thought that everything in the UK – work, family, even leisure had become intense, pressurised and somehow desperate. She tried hard not to let events at work phase her. They only happened every now and then after all. Most of the time people were polite and grateful for clean toilets – most likely grateful that somebody else would do this shitty work. Mostly though it was just cleaning that she was required to do.

Waking again in the depths of the night to hear her husband return late, she recalled fights that she had with her brother as a child in India – the way she pinned her squirming brother down between her strong thighs. "Thunder thighs," her father teased, but they came in handy every now and then. In the bed, she sighs deeply and sees it as her fate in the world to daily turn shit, ugliness and mess in to order, cleanliness, grace and goodness. When she had been a small girl in Bangalore her father had said that it was good to take pride in even the smallest acts or tasks – the intention was everything. In her own small way she liked to think she was upholding the health of the mighty commonwealth. The common wealth had been a topic she had learned at school alongside Indian history. Everything was connected after all and even her unseen labour served a purpose, surely. She gets up and warms the macaroni and chips in the oven.

That's Just The Way It Is Baby

The voice is softly spoken, but there is dynamite hidden within it. Takes a trained ear to hear it. Donald Duguid's been working as a computer programmer for The Institution quite near the hated Scottish Parliament building for over twenty years now and has carved out quite a wee niche for himself. He's in to niche markets alright; in to cracks. Twenty years in the hamster run, he's been shuffling this data stuff fast from A to B. Bits and tits and bytes from both. From here to there these inscrutable yet predictable codes. And back again to this particular office-orifice to be processed, checked, scrutinised. State stuff, official data, commercial stuff. Records, information. Don't blink now but it's *The Lion-Wolf Man* coming to a candid camcorder near you, very very soon folks. His office desk-den is darkly lit alright, the ego the size of Canada.

Long legs, nimble. Savile Row shirts, classic stuff: looks like a gentleman but isn't. Daddy long legs, used to getting the leg over, definitely as a part time job pal. Legs eleven. Seventy seven. Way to go man, still at it. No need for Viagra, me. Feel them out, sense the vibes. If necessary circle the potential mate physically in ever decreasing rings; then lunge in for a surprise watching her giggle excitedly. Donald Duguid's a fast mover with the women, like. The technique's worked well on many women in the building and out. Smoozling, phubbing, fibbing, spinning, grubbing and hustling. Pitter-patter, flatter, smooth-as-butter then fuck her. Always hustling, on the look out for opportunity, signals.

Seventy seven is how old da is now. He is still well over six foot. He hasnae shrunk at all. Cheeky old codger, da, is romancing the ladies at his age. Da met his latest *friend* at a funeral. If you wanted someone to blame as a role model for Donald's womanising and liking of the lassies then you could fockin' blame his da; the true seed. Showering again first thing before another day in The Institution, Donald reviews the various components of his PC in his mind. That is the neat thing about IT, you can switch on and off, you can compartmentalise, control. In the early days you could make it up as you went along, anonymously of course. All training provided and paid for by The Institution naturally. That was the beauty of it. Out of one of The Institution's many showers he steps and into the office fray. It's a strange open plan office with no obvious centre of gravity. No matter, the crack today is buzzing. It's May Day, workers' day, have-it-away-day and nature in all its forms is buzzing outside the office walls.

"Great match last night, eh? Exciting game." His comment is flung out in to the grey and black office orbit. It's an innocuous looking 1970s block near Calton Hill, a main road and a mini supermarket. His colleagues, upfront women discussing menopause, pension plans, diets and last night's orgasms up until His Entrance. The office looks banal, grey and harmless on the outside, but *inside,* baby. Inside. Well. You'd better believe it. Just a big gossiping shop. Lots of cubby holes here, private work desk-areas; lots of banal rows of people tapping mindlessly on keyboards trying to pretend they're not going mad with boredom. No plants live in the main records room; the one and only plant struggles to live in the kitchen unwatered. Any kindness shown to it; any wider action taken for nature; any mention of the environment or respect for living things is dismissed in this man made hell hole as do-goody, soft.

But you have to swipe everywhere in it and all email is monitored.

Donald, or call him Don for short, he's a bit of a joker, really. Just a pussy cat. Fifty, going on fifteen. Never say no to a bit of footie, eh? He knew what the women say about him at the other end of the office, the stuff about his very own end and getting it away. *So what,* he thinks. It only adds to his proud reputation. Several times he's pumped and filled them up in garage forecourts, parking lots, even the odd petrol station's been known. That really was a case of pump and go in the go-cart meat wagon. The men who work the petrol pumps near to his home in Leith's Underworld know all about it, like. Behind closed doors they cheer him on. Donald has a private network too: the bots in the botnet. They meet privately and swap stories, photos.

"Yes, exciting game. Looks like Hibs will move in to the front ranks. What book you reading now, Don?" Jacks ask him laughing away and catching the other girls' eyes at the same time. Heck, what was life without a wee bit of wind-up and flirting? Harmless really. Hearts supporter Jacks is about half the height of Don, and it was her pithy wit that had nick-named him King Cock of Leith Dock many years ago. She's got a wee shield on her PC with her footie heroes on it. They socialised a bit outside office hours not just at Christmas. She's married to a long distance lorry driver and can dish it out as well as take it. She knew about his conquests right enough but could be relied upon not to blow his fragile cover to The Wife, back home. She'd really goaded him once publicly at an infamous Christmas Party five years ago in which half the office got pished, mashed, scuppered. *How is the fresh beaver meat these days by the Waters of Leith, Don? I gather it's not just otter meat you can get if you fish around a bit,* she'd practically screamed at Don, causing the office girls to laugh with delight.

They have a flirty, friendly work relationship, Jackie and Don. Jackie, call her Jacks for short; she can take a joke right enough. They get on well these two; almost a double act. He often joked that he wanted her, she always replied tartly with a curtsey and an *"anything else I can help you with the day sir?"* And so it went on. They didnae mind what people said, how it looked. It's only a laugh. After all, most in this awful office have perfected the art of *Brutish-Scottish*, in fairness a language not spoken by all Scots. The whole idea is to club your victim with words: you could hurl spite, abuse, insults – frankly, the choice was yours. Great kudos was to be had for dumping the most toxic stuff too – particularly with a side ordering of acid sarcasm. Jacks loves toffees, big bags of them; along with winding Don up, of course. Don grins.

It's about humiliating the victim; nobody gets away, no special treatment for anyone. Staff here feel free to comment remorselessly on anything; paper is not the only thing that is shredded mercilessly. Either hurl the shit back instantly or go under and start on the booze, the porn or anti-depressants. Maybe take your own life as a way of opting out of the living office hell-hole. Think about it, maybe: then there's no career options to worry about. Endure the gossip, innuendo, snide insinuations; take it on the chin this is Scotland. Else what are you, a daftie? No delusions of grandeur allowed here, *it's strip and nick.* Donald looks up from his book to answer Jacks, who's chewing away.

"Whoarr.... It's Marlon Brando's autobiography. My God, the things he got up to with those starlets in that sunken bath tub of his... four women at a time All nighters. too. Lucky man he was. Shame I don't get invited to any orgies."

"Just you watch you don't spend all your time reading pal. Might not be a good idea at home, might it."

There is a picture of Bonnie Prince Charlie on Don's desk, that romantic Scottish brave heart hero of the Scots who were not always really united. Don has got to load data, send data, organise data fast like, by tight deadlines. Only the best technology will do. He has got to be smart, agile, alert for anything. It's all about performance. Often no time to eat properly, sometimes no time to sleep either. The bottle of lurid blue sports drink, a real ego power aid if ever there was one, sits demurely in the kitchen fridge. Might squeeze a gym work out in later with Maggie. She's always a laugh. Arse not bad either. Maggie works on The Institution's reception. Don feels his shaved head and stares at the fresh stuff to be loaded today. There had been a problem with the IT system yesterday which had taken most of the day to sort. Outside, a distant cloud drifts then mutates gracefully in to a puffy vertical line. Another day, another dollar. Gee Whizz. Where did the time go. *But iclouds, man, you could really get high on the stuff up there too.*

And that night with Scintilla last month though. *What a shaft.* All the action had taken place after the curry. She had performed well for him when he had been stuck between a rock, a cock and a hard place. Now that *had* been an exciting game. She wanted more than an occasional slice, though, and he had to draw the line. "That's just the way it is, baby". She had swallowed it well, his silver lying tongue. No tears before bedtime or even during. That was always his rule. It was tough. *But then again, baby, life is tough.* And his colleagues, well, they all knew about his prowess, his know how with even the high powered female management up on the fifth floor of The Institution. The building is also quite near a huge telephone exchange and interferes somehow with the staff's mobiles.

Now there on the fifth floor, there you had to change tactics slightly. Different ball game. Bright university lassies, pal. A more sophisticated tackle needed. Lunch, a piece of ham flung on a roll, then it's into the second half. Late that afternoon, the office women are screaming at each other again, talons are out. *It's bitch this, bitch that, excuse me this.* Jacks wisely does a cross word, opting out of The Excuse Me Club for today. Even she thinks some hens are bad, like. Give them an inch, they take a mile and she'd knew of quite a few secret high grade slappers in the office. The photocopying machine has broken down again; she thought Don might actually punch her when she accidently bumped into him. But Don held it together well and just put his feet up on his desk; just smiling and taking his time. He can get away with this louche manner as he makes his female line office manager laugh.

Dorothy, the office manager is obsessed with perpetual diets; losing weight and gaining weight. All the office women inflict light to moderate body surveillance on the other women: in the ladies' toilets an almighty pair of scales has been placed by a full length mirror. All hail the scales. So if the security swipe cards don't install intense self-consciousness and tension then the continual hang ups about body size will. But big Don doesnae fret about the size of *his* butt; he's a consumer and surveyor of butts. *An easy life, me.* Dorothy knows he likes to have a little scratch during the day and she keeps quiet about the wee fluffs and the scores. She just laughs and says he's a naughty boy, like they all do, bless 'em. It's all about the score man, the score. Balls in the net, finger in the dyke.

After work, he rings the number. "Hello?" It's a young female voice, hesitant yet keen to explore. Potential game, alright. There's a weird reception though today; he reckons it's coming from the east. The mobile crackles a bit. A few times he'd whipped out his equipment in a public car park; the lassie just chucked a makeshift jacket on the ground.

"Oh, hello. You responded to my advert on Grapevine?" Soft voice, encouraging. Erotic pause. He always loved this bit best. The build up, the frisson, the psychological manoeuvres. *Come on, my lovely.* "Want to meet?"

Driving over to meet her in his car, Don thinks again how easy it is to score. It is still light and sunny; he has these few unaccountable, in-between hours. Life at home has developed in to a total nightmare, wife's out of work and on the demon drink. So much competition for jobs right now. Daughter, ten going on sixteen, wants to wear make-up and hang out with boys. I have spent years trying to listen to her, the other half. *She doesnae appreciate me.* Don has even got google mapping installed and a satellite traffic management screen in his car. In this time, in *his* precious time, he can say what the hell he likes, how he likes. The car has many hidden compartments, a bit like his mind. *Maybe in the end I am a kind of zombie just running empty on some kind of already mapped out programme. Pinch me; am I real or just 4 kinky reels?*

Sometimes they respond to his offer to take arty pictures of them, though understandably of course some are pretty wary to begin with. *For fuck's sake* Don says to his wife – *I just need to get out of the house. Doing a bit of landscape photography, is that alright with you? I'm only the one round here who pays most of the bills, takes care of the home insurance – just little things like that.* Only the select few mates knew about the truly hard-core hits. He has posted the after shots too. He has a credible, affable manner – never mind that the girls at the office say he is Don Quixote, a moral libertine. Get the shirt right, man (Savile Row) and the rest will sort itself. The future? Slamming the car door shut, Don thinks that the future would not only be pink and tanned – in the future we could all be sixty second adverts of ourselves on cam. A bit like a blue version of The Truman Show. *Ah yes, cam.*

Now, getting one of the cam girls to shave *live* as they chat. There's a thought. A whole new dimension. Fresh fluff. And there is a fresh steady little pool of them that only his very best pal who lives near The Links knows about like. Aww, you filthy dog you. You just love it. He grins the grin of some inane Cheshire wild big cat who has been getting away unblinking with this shit for years. No questions asked. It's wonderful how freeing technology is. In its way, a miracle of engineering. He walks into the carefully chosen quiet bistro-bar in South Clerk Street, stooping his head and trying not to crash in to the top of the door.

The trick is to vary it, don't always meet in the same bars and clubs, man. He inherited his extreme height and perpetually lean hungry look from the old man. And it is a hunger, this. A compulsion, a bottom less pit full of bottoms. He knows this on some level but he just cannae give up now, he just loves to play. A bird in the hand is worth two in the virtual bush. An addiction that he never wants to be free of; it's just way too much fun. She's sitting at the back in purple velvet.

"Oh, hello. Are you?"… He never starts with the 'baby' talk yet.

Don't be too crude and obvious; he has to prime them first. Don't give the beautiful game away. The girl looks feisty yet shy. The uninitiated. Maybe she's a student, there's lots to choose from. Recently he'd heard about some bright business starter upper which involves rich business men and broke female students. *Brilliant.* Supply and demand and in this brave new world baby you cannae blame a lassie for using her assets to boost her assets. What the hell was a lassie to do if she were *hard up* for cash? It's rich pickings for all concerned – this jiggling and hustling about. Plenty of dirty instant cash about, don't believe everything you read in the papers. The bar is upmarket, not too laddish and no big footie screen here, thanks. Scintilla had shaved her fanny in to a heart, he had liked that. Touch of class. But then she was an exceptionally good score.

Some lassies he'd gone with went the extra mile and dyed their bits the colour of footie strips. That took real dedication, he didnae know quite how they brave hearted that one out. He'll see Scintilla again soon, as she does such a special little number with the nipple tassels. Such a good range that girl but she's busy working at Peppermint Antelopes, an exciting new two-for-one strip club in Lothian Road. You had to sext well in advance. Tasteful pot plants have been placed strategically around in brass urns, the Edwardian bar mirrors lending ambience. Donald offers to buy her a drink, reassuring her in his charming way that he will not spike it. She's called Penny and yes, she says she's a student. She's recovering from a real toss pot of a boyfriend who went and cheated on her one time too many. *Two can play that game* she says, downing lager.

There have been times over the last twenty years when Don's wife has nearly cottoned on, but he's always lied really well. A bit frightening if you thought about it too deeply. Just how many people only believed what they saw with their own eyes and never asked deeper awkward questions. Don thinks a lot of people are just gullible gossip mongering cowards anyway. And given this current climate of fear and uncertainty with most wanting a slice of something – well, it's each one covering their backs out there – each man and woman at the end of the day out for what they can get and hey, why not off load both your costs and your love-juice on to others who will willingly carry if you cough up something. *Just do it if you can get away with it.*

Don has got his shades and chinos on, he's looking uber cool. Extra long leg of course. He'll try a cheap line in empathy, he'll contact his inner woman – he knows how to do that too. *Thank you popular mass psychology for handing us the language and techniques all on a plate.* Most lassies after all are insecure about their looks, capitalise ruthlessly upon this too. If necessary play one hole against another hole or get them to slag and bang each other and then jerk off over that. All in one self contained session, discretion assured. If some thought *he* was bad – well, two of his mates down in Leith – they were up to their necks in it. Advertise yourself as a photographer with legitimate arty shots, that's just the cover line. *And those politicos were all at it too, Don will not take a bloody moral lecture from them.* If you face a financial black hole as Don knew some hookers did down in Leith then folk used their very own black holes.

Once a very poofy looking IT intern on day release from Stevenson College confronted him over his behaviour at work safely in the men's toilets. *What's your problem, pal – you swing for the other camp or not getting enough?* he'd said to the guy, another part time student as well as intern. Edinburgh is crawling with fresh young student meat. *Nah pal, the lassies I know love a bit of slap and pickle in the*

*morning and some of them are more than on heat if you take
my meaning. They can be as predatory as the fellas. You got
that wrong.*

The intern didnae have a leg to stand on. Maybe he was
on some other kind of day release too, he looked a bit funny
in the head like, come to think of it. Later, when the time is
right Don will slip an arm protectively about Penny's
shoulders. But who knows, let's see how this little number
will play out. Good game, good game. May lead to goal.
Penny looks quite arty, with ripped jeans, velvet top and a
devil may care glint in her eye as she swigs down the
second lager. She is assessing his willingness to pay,
checking him out for slack. Even better, Don thinks. He
likes go-ers; they get ahead and give good head.

*

Don steps out of the shower, the shower at home this
time. In one shower, out the other. A man for all seasons.
My life on cam by Donald Duguid he chuckles softly to
himself. He just loves that lemon zest soap he'd just used.
His divorced mate near Leith Links has got home made
video footage going back over twelve years, a library of clit
flicks. Free to borrow, any time pal. 24 hour library. Police
no wiser, nothing illegal here my son. Recently he'd read an
interesting article about how most Scottish men were not
satisfied with their sex lives – too bad. Mine's fine thanks,
he thinks. They just lack bravado, the thick chameleon's
skin to be man-of-all parts. *Alright, alright, I'm a male tart
and yes men secretly bitch too,* is what Don privately says to
himself away from prying eyes sometimes in the mornings
while shaving away from wife and daughter. I'm just bored
in my job, man. The Scots have always been explorers of
frontiers haven't they? These days anything goes, name

your addiction: grannies, cougars, swingers, teens, groups, kids, goats.

Driving home last night, after leaving the bar satisfied that there would be more opportunity, more openings with Penny – he thought of his dead mother for some odd reason. She had terrified him and his siblings when they had been young, threatening God's hell fire judgement if they stole, played with themselves, gambled or smoked.

She had been a school teacher, but his da a flighty jock-the-lad. A meeting of opposites. He'd been exposed to different attitudes towards sex, two programmes if you like and he knew he was in some way still confused. She had caught Don once behind the garden shed when he had been beginning to discover just how far he could shoot his winkle. His da had just nodded and winked. *Fair play to the boy.*

Wink at the boy's wee winkle, later this will grow in to a knowing nod and a wink and maybe a full blown nudge between grown boy-men with their new toys. There's a lot of it about. No wonder he grew up confused. As a punishment, his ma, a bit of a matriarch, forced him in to a whole month's compulsory Sunday viewing of Songs of Praise. Leila, the ten going on sixteen year old daughter screams from downstairs at him: it is Saturday and she wants help with her homework. Or else.

"Hang on, honey. I heard you the first time. You'll have to be patient. Daddy's just got to have a shower you know, it's just the way it is sometimes, baby. I have to wash or I'll stink out the place and that will not be nice, will it? I will be down in ten minutes. Have you got your hair in bunches like mummy asked?"

God, he hated this parent on the fly business. How did he know all the bloody answers? Bloody boring school girls; make it up as you go along. Chances are nobody will notice. The Wife has gone out shopping, back soon. Another time at work, must have been over ten year ago the now, the Top Institution's Dog caught him zipping his fly in a suspicious way after leaving said fifth floor. Now there was a definite case of the good old nod and a wink. Talk about brief less breathless encounter. *But The Wife and I, we never really speak in real terms, never speak about the many lost unaccountable hours and how those hours amounted to years.* Somehow there is never enough time, what with housework, school runs, money worries. "Wanna go?" he later asks his bored daughter after the homework has been completed.

They are to go to the park later to play. She's a right madam, Leila his daughter, with the same dark hair as Don. *Wanna go, honey?* The line works well enough on all females, young and old. He'd even tried it at work with success so why not capitalise on it in bored moments. His behaviour at home is tightly regulated, he is allowed a few simple pleasures like reading and of course housework. But a lot of things are monitored. *I'm not really free to be me in my home.* He'd felt like skelping her black and blue, The Wife, last night. Very nearly did, too. All those questions about where he had been and why was he so late. She's got a problem with trust alright. Yes, drone, drone, he will do the school runs next week.

Yes, the Internet in the front room is now child friendly, he has installed the software. *Can he please be left alone just to read quietly – it had been a hell of a week at work after all. It is his chief ace card in the living contracted hell that is called marriage.* He knew she would be disgusted by his virtual alter ego, these other hidden hours and pastimes, but somehow this adds to the frisson, the pleasures. The forbidden. Before the software had been installed at home he had even been able to sneak the odd pic in, the odd cam shot. She didn't know a thing about computers and how you can access, slide, poke and hide.

"What the hell time do you call this?" she, The Wife, had screamed at him late last night. Daughter had heard and laughed. Mummy has Daddy by the balls, those bits Leila had glimpsed once by accident through his ancient dressing gown. Daddy had looked embarrassed and snatched the robe back over his gonad bits. Daddy *is* funny. Especially when he does the Red Indian impersonations.

"As good a time as any," he had shouted back. "Don't lay that stuff on me again. Man, you're not out of your tree again are you?" Then the deafening silence. But he refuses to completely tame the Lion-Wolf. The beast man. He won't be completely demasculated by any woman. Fight them off. No. It is a rebellious streak within, his calling card. Born part beast, part of an ancient tribe. It's the clan, man. Like Bonnie Prince Charlie he would go down fighting, the un-castrated lone warrior-romancer with the proven conquests.

Meanwhile, The Wife just does what she always does. *What the hell is eating away at Donald,* she thinks, stalking the supermarket aisles. It is the same Saturday morning, the same morning that Don goes with the daughter to play in the park. *Ever since we got back from that holiday last year.* She felt like she might be going mad slowly, stuck in the house. Then horror of horrors, her own daughter had discovered some hardcore porn in the family inbox facility. Worse, her daughter had seen it. Still, Donald had moved fast enough, saying that he'd installed child friendly screening software. That was a relief. Fingering a packet of ready meals, freshly picked off the supermarket shelf, she knows she can only push the questions so far. Recently, hostilities have entered a whole new domain and she is uncertain of the outcome. Perhaps she always has been. *Would new underwear bolster her self esteem?* She suspects Donald is seeing another women but she just can't prove it.

*

Already Don's roving, restless and talented eye has spotted fresh tail, fresh meat at the office: she is a temporary intern on loan and contract from somewhere and he may have to move fast. She looks quite athletic, with a good eye for colour. Squeeze in a bit of whoopee on the side, maybe in office hours this time. It is certainly possible; The Institute's buildings are big and anonymous enough. You've just got to know how to work it. His line manager sees he disappears for quite some time, but she doesnae know anything about computers does she? There are enough nooks and crannies available for fanny adam alright. *Just time things well and no swipe required.* Don's line manageress Dorothy doesn't mind lad talk or beers stored after office hours in the communal fridge.

Flexi hours needs a flexible approach and a discreet bevy is okay. There's no topless girls in the tea room, though, the bottom line is drawn there. A relaxed approach to management gets far better results. Next month, he's off to Newcastle for a killer match with pals. Should be a good weekend away. The study with the beige coloured walls is his den-at-home providing refuge for a while and there are brief moments of sadness, yes, when he wonders where it is all going. *You have to start from where you are at after all.* Sometimes he thinks his life is just like a film anyway, he's just a zombie guy in a film not seeing the carcasses and whores. But who is whoring who in the end? Nobody holds a gun to a call girl's head do they?

And you should hear the way some lassies speak about fellas, seems fellas can be meat in the frame too. But he has always been a realist, a hard grafter. His had been a tough childhood, with sarcasm chucked about daily and no room for indulgent emotions. It started in the boys only primary and intensified when girls were introduced. Put up, shut up, get on with it. Life of hard knocks, hard as Edinburgh Castle rock. Genteel Edinburgh and shiny reserved family man by day but too smooth, a bit like his head. At night he might become something dark and brutal, like shiny Edinburgh rock. It depended on how you look at it; at what angle. And all beneath a sugary reserved voice. And there were plenty of others, both men and women that he knew of who were playing this double game, living double lives undetected.

But there is no giving up now: the more disgust he imagines he will get, the more flinty his resolve and the more pleasure. Dick shock and awe, cock as weapon, marker of territory. The repulsion and guilt is maybe all part of his psyche too. Look, some lassies like to be humiliated and nobody is forcing them to pose are they? And sometimes they get paid *and* laid. Fuck it; maybe he is sad, lost and empty. But fuck it equally, he will never admit it or articulate it. What the hell do you do with depression anyway, porn is just fun. *The more you score the more they want, law of multiplication and attraction.* Nothing succeeds like success. Right? The women are using the men too, open your eyes properly. And crying is for weak men, for losers, wankers and the vanquished.

Don's just another Scottish man and they can be a tough blunt clan. Some freely admit this but will not

apologise for who they are. Clans have been walking this
land that men stand on for centuries, marking out territory,
fighting off invaders, defending our patch. His ancestors
came from Roth-shire and they were right straight- to- the -
pointers. Take it or leave it honey. Some Scottish men are
just straight forward and practical, they just say it all out
like. Look, porn is about fun; it's about human connection.
He just says what is, what he sees in front of him and how it
is, doesn't he? He has the right to. Okay, okay sometimes
his bluntness really hurts The Wife and the odd slag but
mostly people like it. They know where they are with him,
don't they, and it's better than shoving your granny off the
bus, isn't it? Ay, it's mickle-muckle loads better than that.
He cried once in 1971 when someone nicked his football
boots at school. Look, he's getting on now in years, he's
aware of this. Don's having to look after his old man, ma
died years ago. Might die tomorrow, mightn't he? But the
close encounters, cam and otherwise – they are real. They
keep him going. Does this make him human, zombie,
ghoulish or a vampire?

Look, at the end of the day Don likes affluence, good
design, status, and fine wine – and the house is des res. He
plans the next liaison with Penny soon. She may prove to be
a real bitch when and where it counts. He always prepared
well, that was the trick. Cover your tracks like a hunter. It's
all about strip fuck knick these days anyway, these extreme
times: the screwing physically and the screwing over
financially. Nick the image, screw then sue. Frame, shame
and a way of making sense of where you are in it, man.
Colour me blue in a grey world. And a man's a man for all
that.

Okay, so this sounds bad, didn't it? Look, Don just feels
alive when he's porn-ing it, it's an exchange of energies.
Excuse the techy language but officious computer people
tend to like acronyms, bureaucracy and efficient

terminology as well as compartmentalising, measuring, controlling, analysing. You can do it to people, you can do it to space and nature. This endless stripping, fucking over, nicking, the final total appropriation, the cloning and zoning, the dumbing of the clowns.

The terrible thirst. The looking out for fresh meat that both men and women do. Oh yes, you cannae say that just men like porn that is only half the story. Don knows plenty of hens who call other hens bitches, witches, numpties, freaks and frigid muff dogs. Where else can you play these days – and what else can you play and scratch with apart from cars, cards, gizmos, gadgets, money, footballs?

Eat enviously with the eyes. Own the language you fat cougar swinger. Gape wide with the hole, you can never be thin, hungry or angry enough. Keep them mean, thin as a bean but keen. Sub language for sub culture but at least here there's tolerance and humour. Unlike the rest of the world which feels frankly like it's going to hell in some imposed remorseless handcart.

It has a terrible relentless logic to it, it's a way of re-connecting yourself because you become numb inside, he's a bit like a zombie, is Don. What with all the data, the family expectations, and the dull routine. Where is the wildness any more? Don just doesn't know if he can do the whole man as provider thing for much longer: dad-as-man, male-as-husband, tax payer. Does he have permission to express myself? Maybe this is one of the few ways he could actually in his spare time when he's not expected somewhere somehow. Does this shock you? How will you judge Don now once Great Britain in some ways but maybe always Little Britain in some ways in terms of the awful hypocrisy? Don forgets to feel, he feels empty and restless in the never ending in between moments: the same-y moments in between breakfast, work, supper, kids, car, mortgage, footie, beer.

His technique is so great that nobody really knew the full extent and truth of his habits going back over the years. The hey man yeah tapes, the far out groups, the way-to-go babes. Adult daddy day care. The truth of Don's lived secret double life. Two identities like – one real, one virtual. Just say nice things to him honey, keep it sweet and low. Talk nicely to it, the little fella below, play misty bar maid for him, tickle-me-pink. Plenty of women swung too Don knew, you just didn't hear about it. Hold this piece of paper very close to your ear and what do you hear? Maybe you hear the legions of hungry, angry, demanding, punishing cocks – there were lots of them about, like. All shapes, sizes and ages. Different races and classes. Quiet desperation and alienation. Unspoken and unnamed isolation even within a family home. Yeah, but, no butts.

Plenty of sly angry fannies too who like dishing the dirt and shit on other women. They'll whip a man and a woman, some lassies will for pleasure, out of jealousy, boredom, or for sick kicks. Some lassies are not gentle, you know, it's a cruel myth. They play a double game, some lassies did – bet you never thought about that, did you? Just as you are about to label Don a woman hater, a man with anger issues, a dinosaur. When Don hires women for shoots like, he at least pays them on the day and you should hear the way some of them slag off and cuss other women's canoobies and equipment. They use and cuss just like the men. The truth is complicated. Left wingers, right wingers, left of centre, some unionised and some private free thinking individuals. Proletariats, internationalists, professionals, professors, conservatives. Yes even theorists and some therapists. Some free range radicals left, strutting about for sport in court yards with red feathers marking out time and territory. What's your beef, pal?

Look some people do god, pal. They are born again. Don prefers porn again. That is his choice and it's a different kind of re-newal as let's face it most of life is utterly boring and grey. And it's the same old excuses and glossed over dross from the stifling establishment who preach morality on the one hand but who do the same in the hidden corridors of power. And sometimes far worse. So spare him your diatribes from the political tribes, it just won't cut it any more baby. Fuck the mainstream now, Don wants the underground stream, his own golden showers when he wants. You can't teach some old dogs new tricks you know.

It's a momentary splurge of sensation, of reality away from the intense hypnotic flickering screens which slowly come to eat away at Don and his life. He feels real and it's nobody's business what he does with his money. Gentleman's code, a private individual's prerogative. The Queen has them and uses them, so do we. And some men like, they offer holes to men and women too, it goes on in different places you know. You have to use what you've got or frankly go under.

Screw it, maybe the whole Island is being diddled, knocked about, jiggled about, hunted, mounted then stuffed financially or physically, ace card my son if you do both. Look, it's a gaming culture isn't it, you play the hand you have got. And what Don freely chooses to do in his personal space and time merely reflects a lot of what he sees and experiences in the wider society and culture in which we all live. A chip off the old block, old habits die hard, like father like son. Pass it on, pass the buck, duck and cover then deal with your shit. The shit has to go somewhere, it's everything overload these days and life has become intense and tense. Men and women need to off load and do some down time in up town strip and poke-her clubs.

Remember, we are all in this together. A ritualistic purging, the games or societal agendas of exposure, disclosure, closure, disposal, of steal and reveal, anarchy and order. Formal or informal, official or off-the-cuff, his supply of fuck bots in the shared pooled bot nets were treated well. Don's not into kidnapping, forced labour, slave trades or sex tourism. It goes on you know, but that's a bit much for him. Sometimes he thinks that's all there really is the now: the in – between moments, the allocated time as users, mis-users and abusers for consumption and leisure, work-and-family. Twenty four hour flexi time, regimented hours, turn up and perform. Compete, play the good game, enjoy life. Yes, he forgets his off switch sometimes, a lot of folk do. A lot of people get sucked in to it.

Everyone's design for life. Porn is a kind of perpetual physical make over in a reduced life of abstract make overs and re-invention. And always the same repetitive under currents to all of this: the all prevalent *strip, fuck, nick*. Nothing wrong with a bit of oi and oink-wank in the morning, like. A bit of rough fluff stuff in the buff. Don't miss a trick with your dick or your'e licked is what da whispered to Don once. Thanks, da. You're a true man about the town.

The Desperate Hours

Moira Lightrowler knew her husband had finally left her when she returned to the flat that Friday night in February. For a start, the hall light was not on, and Jim usually flicked it on as soon as he got in from work. He worked as a freelance joiner and Jack and Jim of all trades. Turned his hand to electrics too, though he wasn't Corgi registered, he always confessed. *Isn't honesty always the best policy,* he always smiled – and reassured by this, customers booked him to fix electric heaters and to wield wood. His business had got quite a little name for itself mostly near Glasgow – but sometimes across to the east.

But the marriage had been fraught with anger, drink and fights. Moira knew she had 'a short fuse' as she put it. She had been wrestling with it all her life. She knew Jim was headstrong when she married him, but it was always the fantasy, the romance of having a real life Rhett Butler at home (or so she thought) that had seduced her. They had met years ago in a bingo hall. He was impressed with her tigerish ways with the numbers. Last night had been the mother of all arguments: she had gone for the kill verbally and he had hit her.

It had been a hard day at the hairdressers where she worked near Glasgow's West End. A customer who *said* she wanted blonde highlights, had then changed her mind once the foil wrappings had come off. Moira was good at her job; she had meticulously shown the customer what the colour would look like. She'd felt the irritation rise up in her like hot molten lava; the lady had already been a bit hoity toity when first coming in. The highlights were the last straw so she asked her friend Jackie, the manageress to take over. She was due a fag break anyhow. She threw her keys down on the small hall table and switched the hall light on. Silence filled the flat. Usually Jim would be listening to the radio or TV or getting his tea. She had come in late as she had gone out for a drink with some of the girls. In the bedroom, the wardrobe door swung ominously open: a load of clothes are missing along with a suitcase. *So that was it.* Stupid arrogant pig. She was determined not to cry.

She would go out again shopping with Karen tomorrow. She liked shopping in town. This had happened before, right enough. Now though, suspicions which had lurked like a corrosive fungus over the last year had come suddenly to a head. He had been seeing another woman, she was sure of it. Every few weeks he'd come back late saying he had a job out east and once she had caught a whiff of perfume. Oddly, she was sure she remembered that smell from somewhere. Spicy and exotic. Full of eastern promise. Pouring herself a large vodka and orange, she stared at the thick creamy whirls on the artex ceiling. The encrusted whorls reminded her of the decorations on their wedding cake icing. It's been a long painful haul. Moira's blue-black magpie hair tones gleamed in the muted light of the lamp by the sofa. Black, icy and desolate outside.

*

Karen was a really good pal, a fabulous hen. She listened sympathetically in the café over frothy coffees. They were near George Square in a fancy little Italian place. The windy, sludgy rain and the oppressive grey sky paled in to insignificance. A few shoppers scurried by, braving the elements.

"Will you go for a divorce then?" Karen asked, bold as brass. Moira always liked that about Karen: a true Glaswegian, she just came out with it. No standing on ceremony with her. Breath of fresh air.

"Hell, I just don't know. I'm sure he is seeing someone else. Maybe just calm down for a while, eh? I've had it though, Karen. Even if he calls me today, on the mobile. That's it. It's gone on for so long."

Moira remembered all the times she had to cover up the bruises and scratches with make up. The shame of it. She is exhausted; the all consuming anger ate all her energy.

"Have you spoken to your ma yet about this, Moira? I know you two have an iffy relationship but she might give you good advice. She's been through it herself, after all."

"Not sure that's a good idea. She winds me up when I'm feeling a bit wobbly. I know she's me ma and all that – but the fact is she can be a right old bitch when she wants. She's not always this sweet little older lady you know, Karen. There is another side to it. I grew up with her, remember. She's in her late sixties and wears fishnet stockings. And this is in quiet little old Musselburgh town! Yes, and why shouldn't she wear them – I know. She should wear what she wants. Look, what I'm saying is this. She's got a funny side to her. When I was growing up she was more like a sister than a ma you know. Cannae really explain it."

"Maybe just leave it then, if it's going to cause you more stress. See what happens today, if he calls. Just take this time, Moira, to see what *you* want. Have a rest, eh? You must be knackered right enough now."

The chat moved on to Kevin, Karen's eldest. He was fifteen and was truanting from school. If it goes on much longer they reckon they might get some kind of parental court order filed against them, Karen said. And John, Karen's husband, was having a hard enough time at work right now as it was. It never rained but it poured. The rain and wind has eased off a bit now so they wandered near Sauchiehall Street, out for bargains. Seagulls swooped and kept close beady gull eyes on any discarded scraps. Their cry is primeval, raw in tooth and claw. Once, Moira had seen a gull peck and pluck a pigeon to death. Feathers had flown everywhere. The trees were bare except for the ubiquitous plastic bags trapped seemingly forever in branches. Strange fruit. Unnatural. Karen has borrowed a book from the library for her college course so they head up to the library front doors. Waiting inside by a window, Moira saw what looks like brown plastic cassette tape entangled in metal spikes on the window ledge. An ancient faded Ribena carton is nearby, the lettering and logo only just decipherable. It must have been there for ages.

*

It was dark again when she returned back to the flat. Slowly, a growing nameless unease ate away inside her. She could not put her finger on it. When she was a child she had been terrified of black empty spaces: the unknown abyss behind unknown doors. Tunnels. Even the Glasgow Underground at one point. She snapped the lights on along with some music. He hadn't called today and she wasn't really surprised. Probably with the woman now. She poured herself another vodka and orange. Sod the bastard. She had spent years clearing up after him. The sex had not lived up to her expectations either. The vodka is nearly finished. In the bedroom there is a strange bereaved feel. Noticing a pile of his business invoices, a sudden gleam of spite entered her eyes. Burn them. That will *really* fuck up his finances. He won't have a clue what's been paid and what not.

She delighted in the thought of Jim harassing customers who had already paid. Think of the stress. She heated up the oven and shoved the whole lot in. Served him right. Pirouetting drunkenly but joyfully around the front room, she remembered her ballet classes when she was around eight or nine. That was *one* thing she was really good at; she had the right build for it. Even now, in her late forties, she retained a slight but supple physique. No scrawny turkey neck or arms on her, thanks. At one point she became so good she had won prizes but there was no money for professional training. In the end, the pressure of being a working class hopeful being raised by a single parent was too much. That was her first real knock back.

The *Clansmen Inferno* smoke alarm beeped and flashed in to life as she crashed in to the sofa. A terrible smell was coming from the kitchen. Yanking open the oven door, she deposited the crackling papers in to the sink and ran the cold tap. Shit. There were plastic ring binders in there. No wonder. She pushed open a window and the smell slowly subsided.. Evening dragged on. She moved on to the bloody Marys, hoping to drown out the returning unease. Nothing good on TV. Lying awake late, she wondered if she should visit her ma tomorrow. Might take her mind off it. She will call tomorrow morning and get the train across. *It is true,* she thought. Saturday night was the loneliest night of the week.

*

During the long night the vodkas worked their black corrosive magic and Moira was violently sick and feverish. Great globs of evil looking yellow and green bile erupted from her. She had pushed the boat out too far. Never mix your drinks.

"You gonnae be in later today, ma, if I come over and visit?" Moira asked the next morning from her old mobile. It used to be Jim's but he gave it up for a newer, flashier model.

The voice on the other end of the line sounded far more distant than Musselburgh. Ma sounded testy, cautious. A washing machine could be heard in the background. It was not a great line, but then again communication between mother and daughter had always been patchy. Pause.

"You got company, ma? If it's not convenient I can always come next Sunday. I know you go to Bingo some Sundays."

*

Moira got into Portobello early afternoon. Her ma said she would not be in until later anyway. She can literally walk along the sea front all the way there. So there was an hour or two to fill or to kill. It is a bright clear winter day; the sea looked as if it is frozen solid in to pink blue ice. In a pub along the sea front she spied a lone man having a quiet drink.

"What's your name, then pal? You look anxious."

The man was married and shy. He gave short restrained answers to Moira's edgy stream of questions. She just doesn't want to take the hint. Then his wife arrived who was a bit more chatty.

"I'm a bit worried about your husband. Are there mental health issues?" Moira whispered to the woman, a complete stranger. When she felt anxious she always pushed the boat out too far and tested folk to their limits.

Luckily, the woman was not offended and laughed the comment off. It's just that they had money worries at the moment, she explains. Moira asks her name and offers to buy her a drink. The woman hesitates, catching her husband's eye. Probably harmless enough. Just a bit lonely. Moira returns from the bar with two drinks and glances again at her mobile phone.

"You seem popular," the woman says. Throughout the conversation, Moira's mobile had received two texts.

"I used to be a ballet dancer, you know" Moira white lied. "What's your mobile number then? I'd like an extra friend."

The couple got completely spooked by Moira's hungry over friendliness and politely left.

*

She knocked loudly at the door. Finally, her ma opened it. She was fully made up with blood red lipstick. And there it was again: that exotic pungent perfume she had smelt on Jim. The two women looked at each other and in that terrible awful moment Moira saw again a horrifying black abyss, this time in her own mother's eyes. Years fell away. Her mother tried to shut the door but Moira, realising the deceit, put her foot behind the door. She screamed 'bitch' but the door was slammed in her face. Hot desperate tears streamed down her cheeks. So that was it. It had been going on for a year, maybe more. With horror, Moira realised she has never really known who her mother was. For some reason she suddenly remembered the looks her mother used to give her when she had won the awards for her ballet. It was a similar look. Moira's stomach lurches violently then in recognition. In the enveloping darkness she wandered blindly towards the cold sea. All those years it had been hidden, forgotten. Buried. All that was left now was the need for release. She had spent her whole life dancing alright – dancing with her mother's shadow. She only saw it now. Softly, it began to rain and it seemed to her that the water could somehow absolve her, take her to a thankful oblivion free from the horrors of existence. She walked on, a straggly kind of washed out crow suddenly able to see even through the salt spray and relentless tears.

It was the council cleaning workers who next morning discovered her body swaying gracefully in the waves as if caught up in some kind of perpetual rhythmic dance.

The Photograph

Endless puffy snow falls down from the sky turning the whole world white. It has been falling for hours now, muffling out everyday sounds and somehow cleansing life of its sins. And somehow time is temporarily suspended and there is a steady kind of blanketing out of the mundane, lending itself to introspection and hidden possibilities. Past is present and present is past: perhaps listen instead to the silent white noise that permeates the ether. Lying ill in bed, Natalia, PhD anthropology student, contemplates both her lot in life and her thesis. In the silence she concludes that something is often missing in the rational western civilised mind. It had started snowing last night but they never thought it would actually settle. For now, the competitive hot house of academia is far away.

She had been giving a tutorial yesterday morning to some rather tedious under grads when the first sneezing and coughing began. The tattoo on the top of her left arm had begun to tingle: this is always a tell tale sign that something was wrong. A kind of advanced warning system. Or emotional radar. She only got the tattoo a year ago as a dare when Ben had egged her on during a dirty chocolate filled weekend. In the tutorial they had been discussing tribes in West Africa and the way the milk tree is venerated as a kind of sacrificial female fertility symbol. Her magnum opus is to compare the use of African and western fertility symbols. She is formulating ideas, taking intellectual risks.

Restlessness sets in quickly though. It is *so* boring being ill and feverish and being sprawled out in bed like an irritable beached seal. She clicks on the radio and hears crackly foreign radio stations. Now grief and sombre Polish music fills the room as details of the death of President Lech Kaczynski and many others near Smolensk in Russia emerge. *We are haunted by the ghosts of the dead* cries one distraught Polish peasant woman engulfed by tears. You can hear the tight lipped reporter struggle to contain himself:

"Some argue we have terrible national flaws: fatalism and dangerous desires which do not mix well with sentimentality. But today forensic investigations are being held to examine why it is that the pilot saw fit to land in dense fog despite repeated warnings."

The reporter regains his professional control. Natalia tuts and clicks the radio off. So what is new, she thinks? Somehow, Poland will have new leaders so, *Jakoœ to bêdzie* she mutters to herself, stumbling downstairs for brunch. Somehow things will work out. But over burnt toast her thoughts return to wars and death and sacrifices. Magdalena had also made sacrifices and worked hard. Ah, Magdalena. The legendary brave grandmother I never knew but heard so much about. She suddenly remembers then the old grainy, glamorous black and white photograph. Surely it must still be in the box they kept under the stairs.

*

Endless puffy snow falls down from the sky turning the whole war ridden world white. It has been falling for hours now, muffling out everyday sounds and somehow cleansing life of its sins. For now though the camp is silent – but Magdalena knows this will not last.

"Stand up when I am talking to you" the guard shouts. Another guard standing nearby laughs. There are just the three of them in that forsaken room devoid of light. She is terribly cold in her thin blue cardigan, but she stands up immediately in the room with peeling, flaking wallpaper. The cardigan has miraculously lasted through four hard Polish winters. She is so hungry she feels she may faint at any moment. Hide the tiredness, hide the fear. Outside, in the darkness and the relentless snow the night patrols' heavy boots can still be heard crunching their way around the dark blocks of the ghetto. Always be alert and ready, never complacent. Just like *they* had been taught to be. Both hunter and hunted obeyed the rules of the ghetto: both were bound and implicated together in strange ritual. Only the other day one had tried to escape, Mr. Liebowitz, the barber. He had broken the rules of the ritual, of the order. So they shot him half way up the fence and he had hung there like a startled rabbit, dripping blood. Left as a warning.

And there are the quiet whispers of deaths more awful than this, of hidden camps in distant woods. The lights had gone out an hour ago, strictly according to orders. Magdalena takes a silent deep inward breath. She always did this on fortnightly inspections, it is a silent prayer. *If only the adjustments on the uniforms are good enough to satisfy* she thinks as the guard stamps around the dummies and the samples. Show no fear and never assume. They appreciate humility and quiet hard work. He seems satisfied with the work and comments to his colleague. Lately, it has been hard to sew neatly as one of the light bulbs has blown. The two men laugh then, eyeing her tremulous body and her golden curls. Keep very still and all will be well. Maybe the war cannot go on for much longer, she had heard whispers in the ghetto about Russian conquests in the East. Some of the guards had been called away to fight.

"Pretty for a Jew, huh," the soldier leers at his comrade. The two men look knowingly at each other and then at

Magdalena. Her heart pounds. She can hear the men breathing heavily. Now she is the rabbit, the hunted one. She looks at the ground. The officer locks the door and reaches in to his grey coat pocket for a bottle. Before she can scream one has bound her mouth and the other has forced her to the floor, pulling off her threadbare clothes.

*

On the radio there is a bizarre story about Uri Geller wanting to buy up an Island in the Firth of Forth as he thinks there may be ancient Egyptian cutlery buried there. Natalia laughs out loud. That is the really great thing about Edinburgh, she thinks – so many unusual people live here. She and Ben met at Uni and had settled easily in to Bohemian life near the Old Town. There had been some right old heart wreckers in old Reekie in the beginning, when she first moved up from London. Ben is such a sweetie, he fixes everything well in the bicycle shop he runs. He even fixed and mended her broken, fiery spirit when she had been recovering last year from a miscarriage and screaming telephone rows with her mother Anna in Łódź. They had been trying for a baby for over a year now with no success. She leaves the washing up, feeling tired again. Outside the snow has stopped but a strong wind has sprung up seemingly from nowhere, forcing trees in the street to sway and creak under pressure. She finds the photograph in the box under the stairs, buried amongst piles of dusty papers and albums. The face that looks back at her through time is pure Slavic beauty: all graceful lines, Hollywood tresses and dark intense eyes. The eyes shine with trust somehow; a smile curls around the soft full rosebud mouth. *Magdalena.*

You were an innocent and my mother thought the world of you. I am so sorry I never knew you, but I heard practically everything about you. Your trials and struggles. How you outwitted the Nazis and retained your dignity. They never sent you to the gas chambers because you were so good at repairing and making uniforms, your nimble fingers and your wits saved you. You took risks and survived. I have inherited my fiery independent character from you and my mother. After the war you set up a small tailoring business and met and married my dearly departed Grandfather. Times were hard in the fifties, there was now a new permanent cold war, never mind the rations and harsh Polish winters to be got through. Immediately after the first war though you had to wash and rinse your clothes in an old bath and take in ironing to earn a crust. You met Grandpa on a farm, romantically enough. Little Anna arrived soon after. And the rest, as they say, is history. You died quite young, my mother buried you in Łódź. Of course I cannot hear now, first hand from your lovely rosebud mouth, those stories from the glory days and this makes me sad. As far as I know you took no secrets to the grave. Marma says you even had a premonition of your own death; you saw a luminous light one day emanating from a tree. It was Marek calling you to join him you said. Jakoœ to bêdzie. Then a magpie landed in the tree and the unearthly light dissipated. Soon after you too left this world and your daughter Anna almost died herself with grief. Let me tell you, Magdalena, the world is still up to its own tricks, you are not missing anything. Now we have a new horror, grandma: the horror of a warming polluted world. Believe me, it is another kind of war being waged but we Poles still risk all, enflamed with passions from the past. Only recently President Lech Kaczynski and many others near Smolensk in Russia died in a tragic accident. Are you turning in your grave now, Magdalena – oh where are you gone to best beloved?

"You still up Nat? Naughty girl. Doctor said you should rest."

A powerful freezing wind blows straight through the house as Ben struggles to slam the front door shut. Natalia blinks herself awake in the darkness. With a slight shock she realises she had crashed out on the sofa for hours. A snow covered Ben clicks on a side light, looking like an explorer from the arctic.

"Hey, sleepy head. You up for some warm bacon rolls?"

Magdalena never spoke about the rape or the burning shame she felt lying on the floor in that darkened room with peeling wall paper. She had been lying there all night. Sofie, the young girl who helps with sewing and mending realised what happened and starts crying as she knelt to dab cold water on the purple bruises on Magdalena's thighs and face. Her body ached terribly and her flimsy dress had small flecks of blood. Slowly, with Sofie's help, she sits up. She becomes aware of a throbbing sensation around the area of her birthmark on the top of her left arm. Later, both women say she simply fell in the dark and bruised herself. Meantime, work must go on. It is the thing that gives them certainty and meaning in this seemingly endless tunnel of warfare.

As the days grow lighter it becomes obvious though that she is pregnant. It is impossible to disguise the growing bump and pregnancy could be moral and physical weakness in a worker. Luckily, the ghetto is so cold even in spring that all prisoners, workers and guards wear huge blanket like bulky coats which help perpetuate the deceit. One awful night in July Magdalena miscarries behind a huge shed full of tractors and farm machinery. The small under developed girl is buried in a stretch of woodland just inside the ghetto grounds. They name her Marta, saying solemn prayers for her soul and laying a few discrete wild flowers upon the freshly dug soil. It is excruciating to walk away from the sunlit trees, to not turn one's head back in regret.

Finally the war is over and the ghetto is dissolved. People huddle together pulling wooden carts and horses back to their beloved villages and towns. It is a long road back to sanity, to the good life.

"Jakoœ to bêdzie, my dear loyal friend. Until we meet again. Be sure to write to me."

Sofie, a city girl, is to get the next train to Warsaw. They are standing on a small platform at the train station. The women look deeply in to each other's eyes – each holds the other's history in their heart. Magdalena begins work then on a farm on the outskirts of Łódź and soon catches the eye of handsome farm worker Marek. They take a day trip in to the city one glorious day in Autumn and each have photographs taken partly for official work requirements but partly as indicators of growing affection. Marek snatches the photographs from her nervous hands admiring his brown eyed blonde's luscious curls. The eyes that look directly out at him shine with trust and a playful smile curls around the soft rosebud mouth. He kisses her cheek.

*

It is snowing heavily again and the ferocious wind which had begun several hours earlier is showing no sign of stopping. Everyday traffic sounds are muffled out: listen instead to the silence for maybe it has its music too. Natalia recalls then a strange unearthly dream she had been having of light filled trees and beautiful wild blue flowers. She is angry as Ben had rudely awoken her.

"What the hell are you doing you idiot," she shouts as Ben opens the back door out in to the yard, trampling around in the deep snow like a mad puppy. In one treacherous gust the precious photograph is swept from the kitchen table out in to the swirling abyss.

"Christ, no!" Natalia leaps out blindly in to the freezing torrent pawing frantically but it is too late. It has been taken by unknown forces. Silence. Suddenly, without warning, she begins to wail as a huge wave of grief catches up with her forcing her to double up in agony.

"You bloody idiot. That was the *only* photo I had of my grandma."

She is hysterical – all cool academic reasoning flown out the window. Later, when the storm is over, Ben is sent out in to the yard on a mission to find the photograph, but no luck. In one last desperate act of remembrance she rings her mother in Łódź. The line is crackly but she can still decipher her mother's voice.

"Natalia, I have a copy of that photograph you describe. It is alright. I will send you a copy."

Pause. Natalia describes then the strange dream to her mother about the trees and the unknown blue flowers.

"Marma. Is there something you are not telling me?"

Anna tells her then about little baby Marta, about the sister and aunt they never knew. *I had been waiting for the right time to tell you.*

Three weeks later, Natalia discovers that she had not been ill as such. She is actually pregnant again. A copy of the photograph arrives soon after which somehow reduces the shock of this discovery. When a little girl arrives nine months later they name her Marta as *Jakoœ to bêdzie* – somehow things will work out.

Through a Glass, Darkly

Christopher Cudd is riding his bicycle at night feeling alive and primordial. It is always a communion with the basic elements for him, a stripping down to the essence of things and he momentarily forgets the grey day time existence as a civil servant. *I am an independent warrior and nobody can touch me. I am free to come and go as I choose. Invincible king of the road. See me as I flash and duck and dive through the night, niftily outwitting those overweight dullard car drivers. I am here and I am there but then I am gone. Catch me if you can. The human fire fly, that's me: I dazzle with my speed and wit yet still you cannae really see me – I'll make sure o' that. I may be a small man but you cannot fail to notice me as I move so deftly, do I not? My calves are up for it: I enjoyed a real sweaty work out with one of the girls earlier in the work gym. I am faster than the speed of light and nothing and nobody gets in my way, ever.*

As a child he had loved the cartoon character Road Runner who outwitted everyone on the road. Feeling his arms and legs work overtime as they pump through the rushing damp November Edinburgh air, Christopher can beat time at its own game and escape. After all, these days life seems to be about endless rushing and devising the art of getting away. Stopping suddenly at traffic lights, the flashy silver chrome wheel spokes glisten, motionless in the darkness. Today had been a hard testing day: lots of deaths to register and classify and of course there is a new English temp woman in the office. He had been watching her arse all day, fantasising about giving the arse one. She had been close to tears so he had whispered slyly to her, warning her softly not to cry. Tears from women always leave him cold, they are usually ploys. He knew he was making the woman uncomfortable and fearful – but what the hell, these little psychological games give extra thrills.

When Christopher retires early next March he knows his colleagues will miss him as much as they'd miss a hole in the head. It is all to no matter though, for he has a plan. He can and will escape. He is a man going somewhere; he has been working it all out for years. Some of these early retirement deals you can get are fantastic. *Also, you may die tomorrow, so always have a Plan B*. But right now he must keep moving, moving through this heavy traffic pile up so he can get to the casino with the little built in dinky slinky Chinese take away which does such succulent spring rolls. Come to think of it, the young Asian waitresses were quite dishy too. Locking the designer bike safely in the casino car park, he chuckles as he recalls the way he had earlier given Jane the veritable Angel of Death and Keeper of Records, a shock by appearing suddenly behind her through a rarely used back office door. Keep them on their toes.

Road Runner of course had been turned in to a musical at one point and smart old rabbit that he is; *he* had suddenly appeared on stage through trap doors giving the audience a funny bunny thrill. The casino is way out in the western outskirts of the city: an up and coming casino catering for the aspiring and reckless. To the muted sounds of fast motorway cars one could do the hell what one liked with one's money and bugger the moralisers. Damn society and its hypocritical Game of Moral Outrage: that game sure made its profits too. Christopher really loves Edinburgh's orbital roads, he loves *all* roads, highways and runways – it is the relentless possibility and feeling one gets in movement. The possibility of freedom, escape. The bike will be safe right enough overnight, he plans to spend the night with a pal who lives nearby so he can safely have a bevy or two. Nobody will deny him a bevy. Hey ho, another day, another dollar. It starts to rain as he walks to the brightly lit casino door and greets Big Chinese Wal, the ultimate in security guard.

Christopher knows that the English temp girl Sandra who sits in front of him in the rather bland open plan office likes Greek culture and Greek philosophy as she said she studied this at university. So, despite her reserved Englishness they had something in common after all, Sandra The Arse and he. Soon he may tell her about his Greek friend Nikolos who he'd met on his Greek adventure last August. Maybe he shouldn't have come on to Sandra the way he did but she did seem like she was the uppity repressed type. Women just needed a good old rogering sometimes.

Come to think of it, she looked a bit Greek: all dark hair, luminous olive skin and handsome big facial features. Straight out of a frieze on the Acropolis. His line manager let him off very lightly when Sandra had complained about his advances. Now he is coding a particularly gruesome death and trying to figure out precise medical causes from some rather patchy official records. In his twenty years at the Registers Office he was sure that the quality of the medical reports he and his colleagues dealt with had slowly declined. Gentle rain which begun last night had continued with a more violent vengeance this next morning and the data on Christopher's pc screen is as fuzzy and blurred as his post binge blue eyes are. The black gammon had not been a success but the wee run on the cards had been better.

"Bloody doctors. Don't give us the full picture sometimes. What the hell does *that* actually mean, Jane? He offers a document for her expert inspection; half expecting her to say "excuse me, I'm in the middle of something – do you mind?" as she often did. But then in this office it's everyone out for themselves and first come first served. No room for delicacy or even privacy. And sometimes no room even for courtesy in the heavy schedules.

Jane, a rather plump plain woman in her late forties, peers suspiciously at the document and coughs. She is a devout Catholic and wears a heavy gold crucifix permanently round her neck, daily delivering her from evil thoughts. The crucifix does not seem deterrent enough though to prevent her from making poisonous verbal attacks on people. She, like Christopher had come to the conclusion over the last three months that Sandra is a sex starved posh hussy in want of a few good rogerings so she had shot Sandra down in flames a few days earlier. Sandra, a rather shy girl who is actually getting her oats quietly on a regular basis, had remained silent – shocked at the intrusiveness and unable to respond quickly enough to the rapid office fire. Jane's beautiful velvet Scots voice belies the blunt forthrightness.

"Well, Christopher my son, I think we will have to email the doctor in question and ask for more information. If they get bloody stroppy on us we can remind them of their legal obligations, though hopefully it will not come to that."

She laughs in a kind of perverse delight and heads off to the kitchen for a cuppa. Feeling a spasm of guilt, Christopher offers Sandra an image of Athens as a screen saver from the recent plane trip he took. Look, he says, it is no trouble – he can upload the image on to her PC desk-top if she likes. It is odd: he is sure he has met or seen Sandra before; there is some peculiar prerecognition. Sandra politely declines the offer but just then some seagulls who have been incredibly noisy all morning now seem to launch into a frenzy of screams and cries in the heavy rain. Suddenly, one gull flies with an audible whack in to an office window leaving behind an eerie imprint of feathers and wings. "Daft creatures, gulls," Jane quips, sipping her sugary morning tea as she has done for years.

"Dangerous rain, that's what it is," Christopher replies.

Later, the team who work on registering deaths and marriages congregate in a nearby pub and Christopher balances a knife and fork on top of a half empty beer glass explaining to Sandra that the numerous potential positions of the knife and fork on top of the glass demonstrates the numerous potential opinions and outlooks on life. *It is all a matter of perception, he finds himself saying. Is the glass half empty or full, and all that.*

"I have nothing really to keep me here in Edinburgh," he further explains.

"No commitments or ties. I really just want to travel and see the world more. In two weeks I'm off to Greece again to visit my mate who is a fisherman in Piraeus. We have become pen pals over the last year, you see. I just want a simple life, me. Doesn't take much: olives and wine. The flat back in Gorgie is just a holding station. Here, what do you see in this glass? A life half lived or a life yet to be lived?"

He offers Sandra the glass to look at but she doesn't care much for this liquid philosophy. She listens politely but privately thinks Christopher a curiously empty man – and yes, as empty and mundane as his glass. Her colleagues keep a watchful eye on her and on Christopher amongst the pub post-work banter. He remembers his bike then, still locked at the casino car park. Christ, and in this rain too. Better get off and rescue it. He makes his excuses and departs in to the night with Jane teasing him about the dangerous rain.

The cave near Piraeus harbour is carved in to the side of an outcrop of ancient rocks. Christopher had discovered it accidentally on his many golden ramblings last August when the sun light in Greece and in the whole of Europe seems to take on some mystical, transformative quality. Ancient drawings of people and animals in red and brown ochre cover the cave's inside walls and there are natural ledges and shelves which once housed religious idols and figurines, according to Nikolos and a rather dusty 1950s guide book he had picked up in one of the tat tourist shops along Piraeus harbour. It was in one of the cafes along the sea front that he had first got chatting with Nikolos, an elderly fisherman who had lived most of his life in Piraeus. They had got along immediately and had ended up drinking Greek coffee and ouzo until the early hours, waving away large grey-white moths that kept flying to horrible all-consuming deaths in the café's many candles placed in the top of wine bottles.

"It is like all of us," Nikolos says, his tanned weather beaten face cracking open in to a sigh and a toothless grin. "We never learn from our mistakes but keep flying like Icarus to what *seems* easy and good for us."

Christopher found Nikolos's philosophical sadness over the moths' doom quaint and somehow alien. As far as he is concerned things live, change and die and that's all there is to it. People's *feelings* about this were neither here nor there, surely. At work, the office girls were constantly getting married, divorced, having babies or attending funerals – yet all this and the thousands of deaths he classified and registered every year did not touch him emotionally. He had to learn early to distance himself in order to cope and operate efficiently as a public servant. And he had been irritated, frankly, by the fuss and emotional outpouring over Princess Diana's death: what was so special about *her* death? It was enough to drive one to republicanism really. And yet for some reason he realised he too was drawn – drawn to the warmth and passion within the Greek people and their culture.

One felt welcomed in to a kind of warm communal bath or spa; the pace of life less fraught – people seemed less in to acquiring *things* as far as he could see. It was all so very different from reserved Presbyterian Edinburgh. It was Nikolos who first told Christopher about the clay female idols which had been found in the cave when it was discovered by archaeologists in the late nineteenth century. Local people now believed that the spirits of the cave were angry that the idols had been stolen: *eidolons,* or spectres of women in strange clothing had been seen since by hapless people passing by during full moons. One shepherd had sworn he even heard ghostly wailing from the cave causing him to have a heart attack.

For a man born and raised in a chilly and cynical City of Reason it was astonishing that such wild fairy stories persisted – yet there was definitely something about this production, worship and use of eidolons or idealised idols that remained inexplicably lodged in Christopher's mind. He saw himself as an individualist, an outsider and even a libertine, and so had rejected the mainstream Church of Scotland outright despite of or maybe even because of his father's disapproval. And yet, in his day job he conformed to ideals of decency and venerated secure stable employment. Sod it though, his sister in Canada was always the favoured one – he was the runt of the clan of the Cudd as his father had always reminded him. Instead, he had briefly dabbled in cannabis and Gnosticism in his twenties, after he had left Aberdeen University. When he got back to Edinburgh he silently promised himself that he would once again read up on Gnostic thought.

*

It is still the same old familiar face that stares back at him in the bathroom mirror, despite the numerous journeys around the world. Looking in the art deco glass, Christopher always thinks that he resembles a desperado if he hasn't shaved for a few days. With a sigh, he sees that the rather meagre beige bathroom needs to have yet another scrub – there are dirty tidemarks in the bath and dust has accumulated on the small window ledge. Of course Judy had liked him to look a bit rough and ready – but that was over ten years ago now.

He had met Judy on in a pub on Valentine's Day just along the dusty and noisy Dalry Road. She had wanted to get married after a few years of going out as a couple but Christopher knew in advance that he would be very unhappy. He had hurt her very badly when he had broken it off abruptly, and in public too – but then no woman had ever really registered with him or *affected* him; no woman had ever really entered his psyche or system so to speak. He never told Judy about the other girls he had shagged on the side and there were some things even his drinking pals didn't know.

For Christopher instinctively knew, even as a child, that it was all about perception, all about image management, about what people *thought* they could see. Fascinated all his life by magicians, he was a great liar himself, even when truanting off school and surviving the beatings at home when he had been found out. Drying his freshly shaved face, the one bed roomed tenement flat looks as it had done for the last twenty years. It is always a big joke with his married pals as to how little cleaning and decorating he had done in it – but then, as he always said to everyone, it is just a holding station. *I feel no emotional attachment to it. It is just a functional living space after all, who cares what colour the walls are. Let them laugh and speculate. They will be laughing on the other side of their faces when I retire in the sun and they moan about nagging wives. Imagine their envy and longing, that alone will be worth waiting for.*

It is a bright Saturday morning and there is no milk in the fridge so Christopher walks down to the local Scotmid. The bike had survived the rain the other day after a tender cleaning but he vowed to be more careful with it in future – it had cost enough. It is parked carefully in the hall meantime, faithfully awaiting the next time it is to transport and transform its rider. He had read on the Internet recently that cycling was enjoying a boom amongst affluent middle aged men but as far as he knew he wasn't going through some midlife crisis. At least nobody at work had suggested it, and anyway he thought he felt fine. He always did feel okay, but he felt even better and freer while he was on the move. He had hired a scooter around Athens last August when he had returned there after visiting Nikolos in Piraeus; he seems to have spent a lot of life on wheels.

Sudden images of Sandra's arse appear in his mind: his libido continued even though he couldn't actually live with women. He felt this was a common predicament amongst men, though rarely admitted. At least he is honest about *that.* Walking on briskly, somebody has vandalised the local bus stop, ripping out the timetable and spraying the word 'debt' in large letters across one of the panes of glass. Bins are often burnt to the ground round here; designed to irritate and infuriate even if you weren't feeling that way already. Spread the love and respect.

Damp leaves, watered by the recent rain, are whisked in to the air by the odd gust. The UK is going down the pan in this recession Christopher thinks. It all happens very quickly then as he crosses Gorgie Road – he had just turned his head to the left and the motorbike just appeared suddenly to his right. Before he knew it the bike had driven straight in to him, sending him flying in to the middle of the busy road. He is half aware of a woman screaming and a car screeching to a halt and a terrible pain in one of his legs. Then nothing.

Jane is on a mercy mission, one of her other specialities. She leaves a large pile of white grapes and magazines on the wooden bedside table. She drew the line at visiting the hospital library for Christopher however; as she was alarmed at his requests for books on new age religion and Gnosticism. All that stuff is blasphemy and hocus pocus, but seeing Christopher look so poorly and motherless with his leg in hoists and bandages softens her a wee bit. She cannae spend too much time on this visit though: His Holiness the Pope arrives soon from Rome a once in a life time official state visit. She sits with him for a while, the over powering smell of rose scented water that she always wears stinking out the place. They are in a men only ward and the young friendly Asian doctor had told him that he'd badly broken a leg: it would take at least six months for the bones to totally mend.

In the meantime, like it or not, Christopher will have to take a break from the cycling and travels abroad. He had groaned inwardly, it is nigh on impossible for him to keep still. Even as a child he had a feverish, restless energy which meant he could never quite complete certain tasks. Quite early on it was thought that there was something wrong with him, maybe even mild autism. Christopher rarely spoke about his family or his father at work; Jane knew his father lived in Aberdeen and is generally cantankerous. Christopher once mentioned that his mother had been killed in a tragic mudslide flood when he was five and she knew he was not really on good terms with his sister in Canada.

He sits up in bed and manages a weak smile. In the next bed a man is being visited by his wife and children; flowers are given to a passing nurse to put in to a vase. A cold mug of sweet tea lies next to the grapes Jane brought. In all the years they had worked together he had never been able to bring himself to drink any tea that Jane made him. He had simply given up telling her he took no sugar. Maybe human connections are merely an illusion in the mind; a kind of continuous tragi-comedy of perpetual misunderstanding and differing intentions, but they somehow attempt more polite conversation about work. Christopher asks after Sandra. Even in his bandaged immobile state the wild fantasies rage on.

"Now, now Christopher – you have got sex on the brain which is a strange place to have it. The poor girl has already been spooked by you enough. Looks like we will be shot of you long before March, then in your state."

Jane laughs. The more direct and rude the language the more she actually liked someone. After half an hour she makes her excuses and leaves. In the natural hierarchy of things God's representative on earth surely came first. Some people at work said that all priests were just men in long dresses – but Jane dismissed any criticism, thinking that others merely envied her steadfast faith. Alone again,

Christopher contemplates going home in the next few days – now he will have to ring the Revenue and arrange an even earlier retirement. That'll be a lot of fun, dealing with *those* vast bureaucratic wheels. Drowsing off before the hospital suppers are served on little plastic trays, he wishes he can cycle again before too long. Big Chinese Wal and all his gambling pals would be asking after him. Now *that* part of existence would be missed.

*

Christopher is reading Jung's 1953 *Psychology and Alchemy* late at night. It is March now and he's been able to hobble about painfully on crutches – but the visiting nurse has been trying to discourage him, saying his bones needed longer. Bloody bones. His bones had never let him down before like this. The long winter months had been a long intense study in isolation and he has been living off TV dinners and baked beans for as long as he can remember, which seems like a lifetime. It is awful just sitting around watching daytime television with overpaid orange coloured presenters. Boredom and frustration had driven him to practically beg the community nurse to trot down to the local library and get some books for him to devour when she had been out shopping for him. A couple of mates have visited over the last few months; *get well, goodbye* and *happy retirement* cards respectively line the mantel piece in the front room back at the flat which Jane visits to re-dust and collect post. What an angel.

Despite being ridiculed and teased regularly by Jane and the others in the office he knew that he was still held in high regard. No matter now though. He resolved to send them an occasional email. New life in Piraeus still beckoned and shimmered mirage like in his mind. Nothing will stop him now from achieving his goal. Chuckling quietly he remembers the giant moths in the café along the harbour: perhaps he too was emerging from a kind of stultifying cocoon. Nikolos said that when the Romans first invaded Scotland they had named it *Scottis* after the Greek word *Skotos* for dark. He would not miss the dark rainy winters.

"Christian civilization proved hollow to a terrifying degree: it is all veneer, but the inner man has remained untouched, and therefore unchanged. Yes, everything is to be found outside – in image and in word, in Church and Bible – but never inside."

Pouring himself another whiskey, he reads on about Gnostic belief. The passage describes apparent identity or 'eidolon'- as being like reflections in a mirror or an image only. Jung then argues that the eidolon can be seen as the ego or as who we appear to be. Ancient Pagan, Christian and Gnostic traditions apparently had much in common and there is actually a forgotten Christian Goddess known as Sophia or Achamoth. In sombre tones, the chapter recounts the Gnostic mythology of the afterlife and the way the Goddess judges psyches at death in the Cave of the Cosmos. Christopher yawns, glancing at his watch. Way past midnight. *Man, those ancients were really far out. Thank God I never had psychoanalysis, nothing wrong with me. All those shrinks are mad if you ask me. Ought to be a law against prying in to the minds of others. Too much liberal indulgent parenting, nothing that a good job or shag will not cure.* Laying the book down in drunken irritation, he heads off to bed.

Isn't it strange the way dreams invariably reveal the hidden? Maybe dreams are not mad at all: it is where the shit and the buried stuff goes – the stuff that is unbearable, over whelming or just too frightening to look at in the cold light of day. Yet it is often in the cold light of day that we merely trudge relentlessly through our days, having compartmentalised our existence well or successfully immunised ourselves from feeling anything – let alone feeling anything for anyone else. And Christopher dreams and sighs fitfully and is miraculously once again five years old, alone and terrified. He is alone in that dark damp awful house in Dundee, the late Victorian red brick one that always was damp. Maybe it is the bricks or poor ventilation but there always seem to be damp patches appearing in unexpected places. It is an upstairs room in his Aunt's house which has a view of the River Tay.

He is there because his Auntie has told him to sit alone quietly. He had started to cry earlier on when the first telephone call came sensing that something was wrong but Auntie had been unnerved by his distress and had told him that boys do not cry. Usually you can see the river clearly but thick grey mist has completely obscured his ability to see through the window. Utter terror at not being able to see the familiar river and he doesn't know what he has done wrong but it feels as if The World is about to come to an end. Auntie has finished speaking to a policeman on the big black telephone in the hall; there has been a terrible accident.

Mummy and Daddy had been rushing back from Aberdeen in their faithful little Morris Minor keen to get home for Christopher's sports open day tomorrow and they have been caught in a terrible storm which has caused rivers to burst their banks. The policeman said the car had been driving on a small country road which simply crumbled away after many hours of intense heavy rain. Dangerous rain alright. Deadly, in fact. Mr and Mrs. Cudd were taken to the nearest hospital but Mrs Cudd is critically ill.

Big sister Laura with the perfect golden plaits bursts in to the room screaming at Christopher and blaming him for Mummy and Daddy not coming home. And now he is running and screaming down the stairs desperate to get away from his demented sister and the oppressive house that forbids the existence or even expression of emotional pain. And he is running suddenly on strange wild open moor land with long grasses, running and running. Suddenly Road Runner appears running beside him encouraging him to keep going.

They keep running breathlessly on and Christopher forgets the awful house and punishing females there. The open space is somehow liberating but when he turns his head to smile at Road Runner he sees that somehow it has mutated in to White Rabbit from Alice in Wonderland. The rabbit has a slightly odd look about the eyes as it grabs Christopher on the shoulder and produces a telescope from its waist coat before vanishing in to some thin wonder-land circus air. Peering through the glass and trying to find his way through the misty moor, Christopher realises that the telescope is in fact a kaleidoscope: now he is even more lost though at least he can see pretty colours.

Waking in sweat at dawn, Christopher feels sick. Crawling to the bathroom, he is startled to see his face in the mirror. He somehow recognises himself and yet does not. The face that gazes back at him looks startlingly empty and in the glass, darkly again a terrible black abyss grows and grows behind the eyes. He is being pulled in to his own mind, a place devoid of conscious light. His lips are mouthing words then; oracle like utterances that had been previously unknown to him, words that just appear out of some nether underworld. *I have lived the life of the eidolon, I am the eidolon of a half life half lived in illusion and insulation.* Foul sick erupts then from his mouth like cathartic lava, but it is when he is returning to bed that a terrible wrenching pain finally engulfs him in tears of grief. *I have been running away all my life.*

The cave seems much further up in the cliffs this time, tucked away as it is in time and dust. Christopher climbs ever upwards in the bright August sun, staggering slightly with his load of camping gear, candles and cheap Greek wine. He had met Nikolos last night and they had once again sat up late in the harbour café talking. The flat in Gorgie has been sold and now he is winging his way to freedom. The leg has at last healed and he reaches the cave's mouth, unpacking his gear in the heat. *Now let the celebratory drinking session begin. I engineered my own escape and survived the urban and office jungle in my own terms.* A far cry from Edinburgh. Slowly a bitter smile grows across his face as he thinks about Jane making endless cups of tea back in that grey turgid office.

The drinking and the afternoon progress together in the Mediterranean heat until a blue and white canopy of stars emerge, filling the earth with those old timeless songs of the universe. A hare springs across the cave in the growing darkness. Time to light some candles. Maybe it is the boozy drunkenness that opens his once blinded eyes to shadows appearing on the cave walls in the flickering candle light. That cannot be Sandra the temp, that's just his conscience playing tricks. He'd gathered from Jane's email before he'd left that between them they'd driven her to a kind of breakdown. Too bad, survival of the fittest.

But then a new horror grows as Christopher realises the looming shadow on the cave's wall is none other than the Goddess Achamoth herself, ready to direct to heaven or hell. In her terrible black eyes he sees suddenly that *he* is now the human moth, drawn to whatever fate she has decided. Engulfing him in her dewy arms she instructs him to cut, sacrifice and bleed. Back in Gorgie, Edinburgh the looking glass mirror in Christopher's flat spontaneously bursts in to a thousand pieces, its false life of reflecting images only now over forever. For what you see is where you are at. And Christopher bleeds in to a place of silent redemption.

Yellow Brick Road

Kirsty Weir knew she has stayed way too long in the ladies toilet in Bath Street, Portobello. Although she's plastered she still somehow sensed the immanent presence of the attendant and their growing suspicion over what exactly was going on behind the closed lavatory door. Taking a deep inward breath; she heard the attendant walk past the row of cubicles and pause outside the one she was currently occupying. She's sprawled in foetus position, curled around the toilet protectively on a cold damp floor. Terrible feelings of sickness and nausea, sweaty palms and every sense heightened and magnified like in a surreal horror movie. Seeing the attendant's slippered feet she's reminded of seeing Tom and Jerry cartoons as a child when one would never actually see the face of the Black woman who owned Tom – you only saw the slippers and heard the voice.

Sounds of glugging water in some unseen pipe punctuated silence; bland tiles gleamed in the strip overhead lighting. *It's a right little whirl, life is, isn't it, a right little roller coaster,* she caught herself thinking, trying to make sense of her upside down world like some myopic new born. But at least she'd cracked and broken down in a relatively clean decent public loo – not some seedy number. A late night car drove past outside but otherwise sweet nothingness, she sensed that night had somehow arrived. And like some fabled creature of the night, some fated siren maybe – she must try and negotiate her way to a bed; a bath can wait until tomorrow. A tell tale bottle of vodka, now emptied of its contents, broadcasted Kirsty Weir's secret little problems to the world. The plastic bag full of hastily packed clothes lay in a corner. Who knows how long she'd been there. A discreet knock on the cubicle door. She might have known she couldn't engineer her own disappearance for long. Ferociously bright, she worked in Scottish Widows Home Insurance office, an impressive airy looking building in Lothian Road.

"Excuse me hen, everything alright in there? I'll be locking up in about fifteen minutes and I'm sure you'll not want to spend the whole night in there."

Glancing at her watch Kirsty realised that this one remaining surety had now conked out on her too; it was the last sure fire indicator of sanity, order – her last connection to some shared reality. Distant fields seemed to call her; maybe there she could catch up with her long lost self.

*

Bright white laundry blows about gracefully in the field on the hill. Once, about a year ago, it had been so windy that one of Mac's smart special occasion ties took to the wind and sailed through the air only to land in one of the dairy cows' fields narrowly escaping a cow pat. Bees hover drunkenly around clover and wild flowers in the grounds of Drum Farm; chickens pick at scraps in a stone walled court yard. As long as the beloved the horses are okay, then Vi could breathe easily and sleep okay at night. The horses always knew if something was wrong, *they are sensitive to vibrations and thought energy* Vi said. *Just like my plants.* Mac Ditty thought her a romantic eccentric but fancied her anyway. She'd been amused by his not very Scottish sounding surname *Ditty* and the odd lines in his namesake too. A big man from the Highlands with wee tufts growing out of his nostrils, Mac is fond of a dram, a puzzle and a good bit of meat, liking his women fleshy. After all, Vi was a good little worker and sold cart loads of eggs to the farm's faithful. For a woman tae, she is a good driver delivering well even in traffic pile ups. Vi is picking strawberries in a decent sized patch quite near the farm house, the fruits are nice and red this year as June has bought the sun. She wears dungarees and her painter smock as she'd been tackling a water colour earlier this morning. Further down the hill Snowflake and Mustapha swish tails, tolerating the flies and summer gnats.

Two electricity pylons grace the sloping field also and a faint humming sound could be heard if it was a still day and there's were not too many passing cars. A farm house has been on this site, this place on the far outskirts of Edinburgh since the twelfth century and the present stone building dates from the seventeenth. At times it's a haven for Vi, at others yet another confining space and when Mac had the builders in a couple of years ago they found a cat's skull buried near the front door as well an ancient Neolithic flint scraper used for scraping animal flesh off bones.

"Look at that, perfect little butchers they were. Knew a thing or two about meat, our ancestors," Mac had said to wind Vi up. He knew Vi was an animal lover and had placed the infamous flint scraper on a mantelpiece.

"All meat is murder, Mac you know that. Animals are living creatures with souls too, you know," she'd countered, having just returned from milking cows. Mac was an experienced dairy farmer and Vi swore the cows look at her with feelings. He'd looked at *her* as if she was away with the fairies but there were tears in his stoical eyes when she'd cracked up after seeing the fox get run over. He always said the stoicism was down to his clan-man complex yet he'd helped her carry the limp bloody fox to the side of the road out of some kind of respect for dead creatures. It had been the final straw that had. Seeing the dead fox just after all the horror and bother at her work too. And it was a horror, lucky it hadn't reached the press or a politician really – but then maybe denial is an industry in its own right. Today's private fruit produce was now picked; so Vi dips a paintbrush in to a jam jar, trying to capture the delicacy of poppy petals. She has to paint to take herself out of herself she realised, but also she must work this talent. It is a free gift in a world of cruelty and illusion. Washed strawberries sit on the kitchen draining board.

June roses outside the farmhouse shook with rain drops. They must be over twenty years old these bushy pastel tea roses and maybe they replaced blooms that were older still, planted by working farmers and gardeners alike. Planted and tended by people who lived close to the land, who listened to its rhythms. It would be mid-summer soon – in two days time in fact. The longest point, the longest day and as far as Mac was concerned, a very productive day and time of year for milk yields. Eggs were really just a side line but they did keep thirty chickens. Drum Farm milk was well known and these rain filled Lothian hills and fields are lush, conducive to top quality dairy products. Recently there'd been just the right blend of warmth and wetness, but Junes could be chancy.

Mac is plodding through thick mud in his wellies, having checked the smart phone for delivery pick up times and orders. None to boot but anything could happen in the next few days and Vi will keep her eyes peeled on the PC when she's not running her brushes, picking fruit and day dreaming. *Away with the fairies that woman, daft as her brush.* He smiles a secret smile to himself as he heads for the vast milking shed. Vi said she needed to take time out often just to chill with the horses, get away from the intensity of the PC's screen. *Could suck you in all day,* she'd cried once having yet another flash back. The milking equipment is humane and he knows the cows' capacity, he's not oblivious to these living beasties discomfort as he grunts a 'morning' to the three young farm hand lads who knuckle down and get on with it over the mooing and chewing. They'd met at the Edinburgh Primary school, her school where she working then. That were over three years ago now and most of the time Vi was okay but her Learning Assistant days had scarred her, no question. It had all happened so quickly, the chain of events both reported and unreported.

"Mind yourself now, that cow's doing the jobbie business on you pal. Serves you right, that's what you get if you take your eye off the pump man. Give it another ten minutes, but no more lads. Where the friggin' hell is the watch you'd said you buy, Malcolm? I'm serious now and I'm talking to you. You need a watch in this job, *all* of you not just some of you. I will not have them over milked at any time do you hear me now? And this is the last time I mention this to you Mal. Being seventeen and taken with a lassie is not really an excuse. Do you want to lose your job? If I get accused of not over seeing my staff or coos properly I get the Government Inspectors filing grievances. Bingo, just like that."

"Right enough, Mac. I'll borrow ma da's watch and get one this weekend." Malcolm, the young farm hand respected Mr. Ditty. What the boss said went. They quietly work on, mindful of duties.

The *reported* chain of events was easy enough to recall, god knows it tormented Vi for long enough. Some nights just after she'd not slept at all, hadn't eaten or gone out. Easy pills seemed to help at first. She and her colleague

Rosemary had seen a bunch of wee school laddies sexually assaulting another boy behind the games equipment shed out on the playing field outwith the school. Vi was shocked but moved in quick to break the bullies up and rescue the terrified victim shouting back to Rosemary who just stood there, numb and useless. There were five lads, all quite big – about eight years old, uber aggressive and verbally abusive. It was a struggle. Vi was scratched and spat on but she drove the marauding pack away. "Please go and ring Mrs. McLaughlin at once – there's a mobile in my jacket still by the driver's seat." Mrs. McLaughlin was the Head and Rosemary darted off looking shocked while Vi rocked and comforted the poor lad. But somehow all the children were still filed on to that coach back to the school fifteen minutes later with the five tormentors sitting not far from their mute victim.

Vi had tried to say something in the stampede to get to the coach and when they'd hit the school at long last she'd taken the poor lad to the school nurse who said she'd ring the parents. Then she practically marched up to the Head's office and asked if any call had been made about the incident. That had been the first deceit and it was difficult to look Rosemary in the eye at subsequent break times. Mrs. McLaughlin denied receiving a call from Rosemary and had "no knowledge" of the incident and furiously ordered her in to her office to explain why two raging parents had threatened to call the police and write to the school governors.

A hysterical witch hunt is what it felt like, unbearable. So she'd resigned, unable to take the institution's sickness any longer. The *unreported* chain of events, the things left unsaid and air brushed conveniently out of public and parental memory – these denials nearly killed her off. She'd been ridiculed as a demented harridan, questioned too – and the incident dismissed as rough play only by the parents of the protagonist boys. Everything she thought she knew she now no longer knew so she ran straight to the safe harbour that was Mac. "Nothing to do with us or my son – maybe some other boy is capable of these diabolical acts – but not my son." Cowardice and lies seemingly without end. An oppressive climate of fear, people just covering their backs and their jobs.

It was Mac who had noted the irony of living in a culture where taking personal responsibility is endlessly drummed in – yet some responsibilities were more personal than others. "It's another bloody animal farm" Mac said reading the whitewashed toothless police report and noting the kind of official politico-legalo language used. The psychological costs and damage to all involved barely registered a mention; it was striking in its absence. But milking time was over briefly now whilst the men took a tea break, pouring hot caffeine in to flasks. Later at lunch Mac will chum up with the lads and eat lunch with them, catching up on gossip while sitting out on warm grass.

Lightning cracked the pregnant midsummer sky open allowing great sheets of rain to descend. It fell on Portobello's sands making elegant pockmarks; it flew in mossy globs in Drum Farm's ancient guttering. It rolled off the horses' velvet backs and added to the thick mud the cows waded in. The heat had been steadily building all day imposing a sense of dread and chaos on Kirsty Weir, who'd twice vomited discreetly in one of Portobello's wee Regency alley ways. Shocking, really. It had come to this. She'd made it out of the public convenience, practically swaggering. But then this was not really all that surprising seeing what she'd had to contend with very early this morning before the heat began building and before she'd crashed out in the ladies' loo.

The foetus looked strangely like a sausage. It must have been growing undetected for months. A bit like the affair Kirsty has discovered that her now-ex Graham has been having on the side. Graham worked in yet another sub division of Scottish Widows; they'd met at an office party defying all the rules about not falling for colleagues. She'd discretely buried the wee mass of quivering pink in the small back garden offering up silent condolences and wishes to the ether, sensing vaguely that the still forming mass had been a girl. She'd always been stoical, resourceful, pragmatic – all the qualities admired in young Scottish women – but she had her limits. The booze provided a cosy whammy of oblivion.

She wears a hooded mackintosh just to protect herself from over curious eyes and there's relief now though as she's nearly off the bus that goes direct to Drum Farm and nearby village. She can bear rain right enough; it just is what it is. They were not hard hail stones and it isn't winter, is it, hen, when the Edinburgh winds that cut through you like a knife came whipping at you savagely from straight over the North Sea never letting you forget your frail humanity. Of course she remembered the way to the farm, it had only been two and a half years ago that she'd stopped living there with her ma Vi or Viv or even Vivian. Kirsty called her ma different names depending upon prevailing levels of trust and intimacy.

She'd seen the emotional state her mother was in after she'd left that bloody nightmare of a school. She'd heard all about it and yes, she was well aware that women in their thirties were not supposed to be living with a parent. The shame of dependency but raw economics and raw family dynamics had trapped her. She passes the chicken sheds and the dry stone walls, having spotted the beloved horses coolly munching on sodden grass. She rings on the door in the downpour, hoping that someone will be in, hoping they will understand and not judge.

"Kirsty, sweetheart. What on earth are you doing here? Is everything alright? Come in. I do wish you'd have let me know you were coming; I'm in the middle of orders and invoicing. Mac's lunch is in the oven, he's out with the cows. But look, I'll get you a towel, you must be soaking."

Vi got her only offspring a dry clean towel. Surviving Kirsty's hellish teenage years had taught her to just back off and allow her daughter to say what she wanted and when. Don't nag or over question. *Try not to panic or be bullied by her either* – that's what that dear Irish social worker had advised her when she'd been struggling to raise Kirsty on benefits as a single mother. Kirsty's engineer father lived more than comfortably in Hong Kong; though devastated by the divorce from Vi, he'd still managed to steer and develop nice little pension and investment pots. Some of this prudence in fairness had trickled down to his less well paid ex and off spring but generosity had seasons too and love is always complicated.

"Mum, it's just all so savage, draining and punishing: the costs of living, becoming a home owner, relationships, office politics at work. Trying to keep my weight down, maintain friends, keep fit, do email rounds. I'm exhausted. When we first moved in to the flat I was so like *sorted* I'd written 'just be' with lipstick on our wardrobe mirror. It was a reminder note to me and us I suppose to somehow keep calm and carry on even when life gets rough."

Claps and flashes of midsummer thunder are right on cue and Kirsty dissolved into a sobbing incapacitated heap. She seemed so desolate encased in the towel, looking almost like one of those poor Romanian refugee women Vi had seen begging on Edinburgh streets – women with sun burnt skin and bits of cloth wrapped round their heads. And the taboo rivalry and jealousy that had often sprouted like some poisonous mushroom between mother and daughter was temporarily forgotten over tears and cooked chicken.

*

They sit at a window table in Spoon Café in Nicholson Street; it's the second time they've met here secretly. It's night time now, candles flicker on all available check topped tables. A dedicated queue of theatre aficionados mill eagerly outside the vast glass expanse that is the Festival Theatre. A Bohemian little place, this café with a nice line in coffees, relaxing background music and affable staff. She, Lucasta, the other feared younger woman, pops small stuffed olives seductively in to her painted mouth. She's a blonde Art History student at Edinburgh University and she wears co-ordinated cashmere a lot. "Everything alright, baby?" she asks Graham who, once upon a time not so very long ago, used to be smitten with Kirsty. Graham's a malleable Fund Manager at Scottish Widows and he'd been unable to resist Lucasta's brilliant line in seduction.

Having studied the use of reflected light in seventeenth century Dutch masters she'd applied this knowledge wittily and had targeted Graham from the start from her Georgian bedroom window which was levelled directly opposite this same window that they sit at now. On the first occasion, when Kirsty and Graham had been eating lunch one day at said window table, Lucasta actually flashed a torch light directly across Nicholson Street from one window to another targeting Graham's face from on top of the brass bed stead. It had happened again when he'd been sitting drinking with a pal one day only this time Lucasta had the balls to wave at him. Eyeing his muse now like some tipsy sailor, Graham sips wine delighted at the ease with which lies can be told, lived and maintained. He's managed to keep Kirsty's nightmare love rival under wraps for several months but then things had come to an ugly head and his online Avatar, his pseudo identity with which he'd and they'd partly co-ordinated and conducted these gutter shenanigans, had been blown fair out the water.

"I do feel a bit bad about Kirsty. I just wish she hadn't walked in on us actually wandering round the gallery quite so entwined, you know. But she had to find out sooner or later. You should see her *mother* if you think Kirsty sounds a bit mad though. A right old hag. She's a semi-retired part time farm worker with hairy legs and delusions of painting glory."

Graham's an ex literature student himself and revelled in decimating people with words. Then again, this growing social sport both real and virtual was not just confined to the City's ample supply of former literature students; in circles they circulated in every one was enjoying have a pop at one another. And it had a terrible logic to it this kind of behaviour – this kind of relentless emotional speculation, purging, identifying and hounding of the hated freaks and the vulnerable. Name, shame, blame.

A kind of restless social market free for all in dysfunctions which, if it wasn't speculating and scapegoating financially could at least afford to speculate and scape goat psychologically under one glorious unified canopy of the "United Kingdom." Those of their friends and colleagues who dared to swim against this toxic tide were all too promptly dismissed as being over sensitive, holier than thou, a kill joy or sexually frigid. At any rate suspicious deviants and, like everything, deviancy and difference could cost.

"Don't feel *too* bad about it, honey. She's not a saint either. Some relationships just don't work and that's it. Did you see what I said about that girl in the gallery restaurant? Who the hell did she think she is, refusing us a table? I'm going to complain to management."

Lucasta seems unperturbed by the devastation she wreaked everywhere – more is the pity as she looks so soft and fluffy. In demure little ballet pumps she'd led him here and there, secure in her right and sure about her future as a prime free range bird. Graham had been blinded and invited to openly gorge upon flesh and fine art and it had been a feast compared to that starved banal office where he worked. In truth Lucasta has turned her whole life in to a kind of living art form and as they leave Spoon for her flat they just don't see what they may walk to. Very soon they could both mutate in to a kind of veneer, appliance or 'app', a self-obsessed and engrossed life style choice, perhaps addicted to the Internet, love, sex, gossip or all four in turn.

Mustapha and Snowball drink water from a trough, taking in the freshness in the air after the intense rain fall a few days earlier. They are quite old horses now and had belonged to the previous farm owners, the ones before Mac. Mother and daughter, two battered outcast women, have surrendered to cloud busting, skies, fluids and white chocolate Belgian moments. And maybe this combination could restore these human husks to the women they once were before others got to them and sucked the living sap right out of them.

"Mum, is it okay to stay for a while here just to sort myself out? I have some savings. Guess it's just as well really. I couldn't really leave before, you know, seeing you in that state. Thought you might totally crack up if I left even though I knew Mac was here. Not safe to leave you or anybody when they are totally trashed like that. I'm scared about even looking at Graham right now; I'm this close to beating the shit out of him. Sorry, does this shock you? It's not very feminine is it but it's real for me right now. I don't want to turn in to a real life poor Scottish Widow festering in Saughton Jail on some murder charge."

"Of course it is alright to stay my darling. You stay as long as you like. As long as you need to. Don't mind Mac but I will insist upon you paying something and helping out. And I don't think it's good you stay indefinitely, I'm not some kind of wizard or witch of Oz who knows all the answers to modern living. It's your life at the end of the day and we'll both go crazy if you moulder here too long. Maybe that's the problem isn't it? Everyone thinks everyone else has the magic answers and formulas. The Wizard of Oz Syndrome but even the self-professed wizard is still searching."

Vi smiles at her daughter, who punches the air and scoffs another choc. Kirsty would bounce back, she thinks. A girl so full of life, with a generous heart. She knew that her daughter would not appreciate a moral lecture on love but it sounded to her like Kirsty had fallen in love with an image, a glossy façade of no substance which just wouldn't cut it long term. There *were* male and female tarts after all, people who promise jam tomorrow and jam yesterday but never honey today. And it was and is so easily done – there were many different kinds of love and so much, maybe too much, importance attached to how things looked. They joked about being refugees from life and asked searching questions about whether the degradation of so many humans was related to the stripping of value from nature too. All this 'news' and focus on monetary value, on austerity, rights, on scrimping and saving for some but excess and gluttony for others.

It is sick, hypocritical and depressing. Vi had problems not erupting in fury over the horse meat scandal. She'd practically given up on the TV whilst she'd been recovering and she remembered the poor run over fox then and knew in her heart she'd always be a radical right enough. She'd bloody die for the right to roam freely even at night and her daughter has this same rebellious streak. And yes, she'd had the jibes all throughout her lived experience – jibes both from men and women about being a canny foxy woman or a free spirit. Ball breaker, dark horse, wild card, weirdo. But also true was the painful messy fact that both women knew deep down that darling daughter had been jealous of Vi's relationship with Mac at first, both jealous of the male attention and protective of her mother.

An uncomfortable mix of feelings, not pure black or white. But Kirsty can deal with it by herself better now, all of this *stuff* that has happened now that the farm provides sanctuary. Perhaps in the end that was what it boiled down to, grabbing moments of peace with or without chocolate. One could go mad in Edinburgh as long as it was ever so *quietly* mad; you still retained the right to this though your welfare frankly was your own risk and cost. And this the supposed Aquarian age, a new age, a third age depending upon who you listened to. At least they'd not resorted to food banks which Vi knew for a fact her former employer used surreptitiously for some families. The hidden stories were endless; the ones that never made front page.

Mac is out doing what he's good at, managing livestock. Slowly the heat is returning and grass is dry enough for a rug out in the open. *Have I really looked a kind of everyday evil in the face and survived?* Vi murmurs to herself dreamily, hearing the gentle slurp of the horses again. She'd been too exhausted and scared for a court battle, which seemed to her to be a new way of the world. It had taken her a long time to forgive herself for what she thought of as her cowardice as the denials and blank dismissals at work. Quite how she found herself still alive after being ridiculed and hounded she put down to Mac and the horse effect. *Where do you go when your pride and dignity has been stripped*, she'd said to Mac. She'd had to actually go and stand near one of the pylons in the field nearby just to distinguish what was in her head and hear herself again. The abuse of power could be so subtle in some manifestations. Kirsty drinks lemonade, for now care free. Swifts whistle and dart high above them, liberated from worry and money. She hadn't told Graham about the pregnancy, miscarriage or subsequent burial. Maybe it was just as well.

"Somebody actually wrote *help me* in one of the school dictionaries, you know, Kirsty, and I never could decide from the handwriting whether it was a teacher or child. Their motto *distribute cheerfully* could equally have been *distribute fearfully* – the Latin lettering was always ambiguous to me."

Vi sighs, allowing her eyes to settle on to some as yet unknown future. Teaching had changed dramatically over the last twenty years; it seemed at times that any joy or enjoyment in the job had been strangled for so many in the blind pursuit of performance stats. Vi had heard of other victims of The System, some teachers some not. They had been gradually worn down to bitter human stubs. Whenever some questioned working practises in the name of humanity, quality of life or even that old contested chestnut 'efficiency' – the same line was often despondently repeated: *that's just the way it is.* Lush and gentle Lothian hills soften the view and cushion Vi's outlook for now, but sooner or later your real self would emerge, your true colours. Whether you or other people liked it or not, what was the point of worrying about some people's limited judgements? At the end of the day we were all just following our very own path, our very own particular yellow brick road.